TWENTY SIX DAYS

A Mystery of Victorian England

• • •

REGIS MCCAFFERTY

iUniverse, Inc.
Bloomington

Twenty Six Days
A Mystery of Victorian England

This is a work of fiction. All of the characters, names, incidents,
organizations, and dialogue in this novel are either the products
of the author's imagination or are used fictitiously.

iUniverse books may be ordered through booksellers or by contacting:

iUniverse
1663 Liberty Drive
Bloomington, IN 47403
www.iuniverse.com
1-800-Authors (1-800-288-4677)

ISBN: 978-1-4697-8604-9 (sc)
ISBN: 978-1-4697-8605-6 (e)

Printed in the United States of America

iUniverse rev. date: 3/2/2012

Dedicated to Maryann Snyder
For her encouragement and friendship

Preface

This novel originally began as a short story, the last of nine featuring Joshua Pitt. Pitt is a young but moderately successful enquiry agent living in 1890s London on Baker Street, close to Regent's Park. And much like many, perhaps most men of the era, he is a devotee of pipe and tobacco.

I had intended to write another short adventure with some finality to it and then simply write no more stories with Pitt as the protagonist. However, in an exchange of letters with a good friend who happened to like Pitt very much, it was suggested I had enough material for a novel, and if I planned to send my Victorian detective off into the sunset, then it should be with a lengthy story and some promise of a future for my character.

That friend was Maryann Snyder and this novel is dedicated to her. Sadly, she passed away before seeing the novel published. It was Maryann who suggested a fiance for Pitt with a wit and intelligence to match his own and it was also her suggestion to move him out of London. Both of those suggestions were taken to heart and have become major factors in the story.

A word about diction, idiom, and language in the British Isles of the late 1800s. Until approximately 1915, contractions were little used. Hence, words like wouldn't, couldn't, don't. I've, I'm, etc., were rarely if ever heard. Would not, could not, I have, etc., were the norm. The exception, if it could be called that, was the use of "nae" by Scots, Borders, and occasionally Yorkshire inhabitants. Would not or wouldn't becomes wouldnae, did not or didn't becomes didnae or sometimes dinnae. There are also some subtle differences in verb or adverb placement in sentences but I'm sure the reader will pick those up rather quickly.

I've made an effort to conform to the mode of language of the times but still maintain readability, and the same is true of locations which are generally accurate. I've also tried to be accurate with reference to money as well, (The average wage in 1895 was less than £150 per year.) so the offer of £20,000 in the story would truly be a king's ransom.

This is a work of fiction. Names, characters, places, and incidents are either a product of the author's imagination or used fictionally. Any resemblance to actual persons, living or dead, is entirely coincidental.

And finally, as the author, I hope you enjoy the story. The great difficulty of writing a period piece, if the author is conscientious, is the amount of research required. Generally, it is seventy percent research and thirty percent writing. So, as of now, this will be the last Pitt story I write, but I do know well to never say never.

Regis McCafferty
2011

LONDON 1895

MONDAY, 30 MARCH 1896

Joshua Pitt opened the door, took three steps inside his sitting room, dropped his Gladstone bag and moved to the sideboard to pour himself two fingers of whiskey. He drank half, then settled into to a wingback in front of the glowing coals of a small fire on the grate. The fire had probably been laid two hours earlier by Mrs. Keating, his landlady, but the Irish Sea crossing had been rough and his ship had been late getting in. He had missed the first train to London and had to wait for the next. The fire had died to coals. He leaned forward, placed a couple lumps of coal on the embers and then relaxed. It was good to be back to his own digs.

Pitt was taller than average at slightly less than six feet, gentlemanly in appearance, but muscular. One might say he carried himself well. His hair was a deep auburn color as was his beard and mustache, both usually neat in appearance

1

but somewhat shaggy after ten days away from his usual barber.

It was the end of March, 1896, and spring was late arriving. It had been chilly in Ireland as well, where he had spent ten days visiting with Pearse and Mairead McCallen, two of the most delightful and caring people he had ever met. After his fiancé, Eileen McNee, had been viciously murdered while traveling aboard the Adriatic to New York with the daughter of Arthur Baines of Kendal, Pitt had no heart for his work. Justice had been done to those responsible, but afterward he was reluctant to take up requests for his skills as enquiry agent.

Those requests he considered serious enough for in-depth analysis and consultation, he sent on to other agents he trusted. And though he had supped with a couple of them since February, he never inquired into those cases he sent their way. It was not that he wouldn't have listened with interest had they cared to discuss them; it was simply that he did not care enough to ask. Close friends, including Mick and Inspector MacLeish had noticed his lethargy, of course, and it was at his urging and that of Pearse and Mairead that he had undertaken to visit Dublin. After ten days and packing on a half stone he didn't need as the result of Mair's cooking, he was longing for the familiarity of his own rooms and decided he had been long enough away.

He rose, went back to the sideboard, poured a bit more whiskey in his glass, and selected an old bent Peterson pipe from his rack. He filled the bowl with some Samuel Gawith Twist Virginia tobacco and returned to his chair where he lit his pipe and looked into the cooling embers of the fire, mulling over what course he might now follow.

Pitt was a successful enquiry agent. He knew as much, as others did. His success rate was high, perhaps not as high as some other private agents, but substantial nonetheless and he enjoyed a estimable reputation. Not to continue as he had in the past seemed foolhardy. He considered other options. He could travel. He certainly had more than enough funds in his bank account to travel where he liked for more than a year. Pearse had urged him to break with England, come to Dublin, and set up shop where he was certain Pitt would be successful. He leaned his pipe up against his glass on the small table beside his chair, stared into the fire and soon nodded off to sleep.

He woke to a persistent tapping at his door. "Come in, tis open."

Mrs. Keating bustled in carrying a tray with tea pot and what appeared to be two scones. "I thought you could use a bit of refreshment after your trip. Were you napping?"

"I am afraid I was." He lifted his repeater from his vest pocket, opened the cover and noted that it was slightly after three o'clock. "But not for long, perhaps only twenty minutes."

"Well, the tea is piping hot as are the cinnamon and butter scones. Two letters came for you this morning and are on the tray. Others that came in your absence are on your desk. You failed to give instructions about keeping the Times and other newspapers but I stacked them downstairs in the kitchen corner in case you want them."

"Thank you, Mrs. Keating, the scones and

tea are very welcome. I'll look at the newspapers later."

He poured himself a cup of the strong Assam tea as she left and glanced at the two letters. One was from Hamish MacLeod and the other from Arthur Baines, both of Kendal. He opened the one from Hamish first.

Dear Joshua,

I hope this finds you well and somewhat recovered from recent tragic events. I was in London week past, and your landlady told me you were visiting friends in Ireland. In lieu of a second visit, I have written this letter in hopes you will consider spending several days with me in Kendal. I need your advice on a venture I intend to soon undertake. I have decided to mend my retiring, and I might add, rather boring ways, to go into business.

Hiram Welch, who owns a small tobacco shop, has been in ill health and has decided to sell. I decided to buy and made him an offer which he accepted. As regards snuff and shag, we have a fine source of product and information here at Samuel Gawith Tobaccos. They, of course, also produce several fine pipe tobaccos and will be one of my sources in that line but I feel that I need to offer wider variety. In addition, I need your expertise in the way of pipes. The current offerings by Mr. Welch are meager to say the least. I would greatly appreciate it, my lad, if you could find your way clear to spend a few days with me.
Yours Truly,
Hamish

Pitt would give it some thought. Much would depend on what demands for his services as an enquiry agent, if any, had arisen during his absence, and if he chose to take on any cases. He took a bite of the delicious scone, warmed his tea, and turned to the letter from Arthur Baines which was quite short.

My Dear Pitt,

I fear that I am in dire straits and in need of your professional services. A serious and threatening issue has presented itself on my doorstep and must needs dealt with in rather short term. I can not discuss the matter in this letter but please have my assurances that it is of the utmost moment and threatens the security of myself and daughter. Please wire with arrival time. Fin will meet you at the station with a trap.

Arthur

Baines' letter sounded quite serious and of course Pitt would assist in any way he could. Mysterious as well, given that in his note, Baines would not provide an inkling of the nature of the threat. He checked his Bradshaw for train times, and readied two telegrams, one for Hamish and one for Arthur Baines, then rang for the houseboy. He handed over the telegrams and sufficient money for their cost with a few coppers extra for the lad's trouble before taking the tea tray down to Mrs. Keating. He told her he would be home for dinner in the evening and tea in the morning but would be leaving on the morning train to Kendal. He was not sure of the length of his stay, but expected to be gone a couple days. He would send her a wire ahead of his homecoming.

Upon return to his rooms, he went to the sideboard for pipe and tobacco. Selecting another Peterson pipe, this time a straight one with silver collar, he filled it with Arcadia and settled in one of the wingbacks in front of the fireplace. Pitt wasn't sure he could be much help to Hamish other than to speak from his experience as a long time pipe smoker with a predilection for quality pipes and good tobacco. He was reasonably certain the tastes of the clientele in Kendal were different than that of Londoners. Arthur Baines was a different matter. There was an undercurrent of mystery and threat in his letter. More my forte, he thought. Well, he would know soon enough. As urgent as the note sounded, however, he was surprised Baines would not meet him at the station himself and was sending Fin instead.

And of course, there was Pitt's memory of Eileen, the woman he had wanted to marry who met such an untimely death while crossing the Atlantic in the company of Baines daughter. Pitt made her acquaintance in the home of Arthur Baines on a case that involved Eileen's brutal husband, and fell in love. Now she was gone. But he had dealt with that ugly mess, or felt that he had, and put it behind him as much as was humanly possible. Fin had played an important role in ending it and given the opportunity, he would talk with Fin about it but hesitated to broach the subject. For good or ill, Pitt had the ability to compartmentalize significant incidents in his life, dredging them up as called for as in this instance, but occasionally disturbing dreams came to visit in the night. Well, cross that bridge, as was said...

TUESDAY, 31 MARCH, 1896

He was awake betimes and after completing his toilet and breakfast, he packed his Gladstone. Almost as an afterthought, he took his Webley revolver and put it in his bag. He would normally have taken his smaller American Smith & Wesson but had been having problems with cylinder alignment and planned to replace it with a more reliable Adams Mark II in .450 calibre. The Webley was heavier but more reliable than the Smith. He hoped he wouldn't need it but felt it prudent to be prepared.

Pitt purchased a first class smoking ticket and was pleased to find he had the carriage compartment to himself. He enjoyed trains, enjoyed watching the countryside roll by as he puffed gently on his pipe. He was not given to guessing, and in any case, there was insufficient data in Baines' letter to even lead to conjecture. It was intentionally vague. There was an undercurrent of fear, however, at least that's how he read it. Well, no sense imagining. He caught a passing steward, ordered a pot of tea and some biscuits and simply watched the scenery trundle by in company of refreshments and a pipe. The direct line ran to Oxenholm, less than two miles from Kendal. There he transferred to to a local that took him to Kendal. Had Baines not made arrangements for him to be met by Fin, he would have simply hired a trap as he had done in the past.

Fin was waiting as promised, grinning widely, and shook his hand vigorously while doffing his soft wool cap.

"Tis good ta see ya, gov'nor, good ta see ya."

"And good to see you as well, Fin. How is the missus?"

"Ach, we mark an improvement since we been here, thanks ta yur kindness, sor. She bin lookin' forward ta meetin' ya, an' has made some apple tarts. We would take it kindly if ya cud visit us after ya see Mr. Baines."

"I would be delighted, Fin. I am not sure how long I will be with Mr. Baines but look forward to having tea with you. Tell me, has Mr. Baines indicated having any problems of late?"

"In what way, gov'nor?"

"Any noticeable changes in behavior?"

"No sor, nothing I cud say as out of place." Fin paused. "Tho he has no left the estate for a week or more. But ya ken, tha' might not be unusual with the shearin' o' sheep comin' on soon an' tother business o' property. Be there some trouble, sor?"

"I am not sure at this point, but if there is and I need assistance, I will call upon you."

"Anythin' ya need, sor, jess call on ol' Fin."

The winding lane to the two story brick manor was of crushed grey stone and lined on both sides by old Hawthorne trees that had yet to drop their winter red berries. The house itself was Georgian architecture, U shaped with both arms extending toward the lane which ended in a carriage turn around in front of a massive oak entrance.

As the trap came to a stop and Pitt stepped to the ground, the front door opened and a smiling Arthur Baines stepped forward with his arm outstretched to shake hands.

"It is good to see you Joshua," said Baines, motioning to Fin to take care of Pitt's bag. "I must apologize for asking that you visit on such short notice but I'm afraid I have a problem that is more in your line than mine."

"That is quite alright, Arthur. As it happens, I am free as air and at your service."

"Good... very good, because this may take some days to resolve. Come, join me for a whiskey in my study."

Baines' study was a comfortable room with bookcase lined walls, desk, and a large, soapstone fireplace near which two wingback chairs were placed. The fire had burned low, little more than embers, but the stone continued to give off warmth. Baines offered Pitt a cigar but Pitt pulled a pipe from his pocket and smiled. "Thank you, but no, I think I will stay with my pipe."

Baines handed Pitt his whiskey and motioned toward the chairs in front of the fireplace. "I prefer a cigar but occasionally smoke a pipe. I remember that you always prefer a pipe."

"Not always. I occasionally smoke a cigar or one of the cigarettes from Bradley's but nothing satisfies me like a pipe. You mentioned in your note you had a serious problem?" Pitt filled his pipe with tobacco from his old roll-up leather pouch, lit it, and leaned back in his chair, whiskey in hand.

"Right to the point, eh? Well, that is good, and of course, the reason I've asked you here. But first a bit of background, personal history, if you will." Baines took a sip of whiskey, drew slowly on his cigar, and watched the heat of the fireplace whisk the smoke up the chimney.

"In 1868, when my father died suddenly, I came into both money and property. The money was significant, but not substantial. The property was substantial. It included an estate and two large warehouses in Liverpool. I was 22 at the time and though I was a manager at one of the warehouses, I was a rather harum-scarum lad. I had my own ideas about business as well as adventure. In 1869, I sold the business, warehouses, and estate, and emigrated to Savannah Georgia in the south of the United States along the eastern coast.

"They were still recovering from their economically disastrous Civil War so opportunities for investment were rampant and welcomed. I purchased one warehouse near the seaport and within a year, built another. I exported only two products: cotton and tobacco, both to England. By 1872, I was one of the leading businessmen in Savannah and it was in that year I met and married Alice MacClain, daughter of James MacClain, a Scottish immigrant who built carriages for the gentry. Two years later, our daughter Mary Fiona was born, named after Alice's mother. We were happy. Business was good and I had a loving family. I had no intention of returning to England at the time.

"In hindsight, I have often thought I should have paid more attention to politics or at least the events of the time, but I was little interested. There was growing social unrest in the South as a result of the Force Act passed by the American congress in 1870. This act authorized the use of federal troops against the Ku Klux Klan, as well as to enforce Negro suffrage. I knew of the KKK of course, cowardly white men who wore masks or dressed in hooded cloaks to terrorize Negroes, but I had never come in contact with them. That was to change dramatically in 1875.

"Between the two warehouses, I employed well over one hundred men, both negro and white, and paid the same wage, a good wage, for the same job regardless of the men's color. My interest was in the business and not in what I considered the trifling politics of the time. If a fair wage and proper treatment made for a profitable endeavor and loyal employees, then that was my sole interest.

"One of my employees, a negro and a strapping lad of six feet and fifteen stone, had a real talent for preparing cargo for shipment. His name was Isaac Johnson, a freed slave who could read and write, and in the years I knew him, he never missed a day's work, save one - the day after his wife Lucinda gave birth to their son. Isaac had a rich, deep voice, a voice perhaps given to singing, though I never heard him sing." Baines paused for a moment, reflecting. "But I stray... I promoted Isaac and put him in charge of our shipping operation, an action that was considered by most of the men as a natural choice, but not by all.

"One fellow, a loud and profane chap by the name of Edward Becker, had much to say about putting a negro in a white man's job and said it often and loudly. Though Isaac certainly heard him, he quite wisely refrained from reply and simply let it pass. I suspect he had heard worse in his previous life. One day, however, Becker was voicing his opinion to all around him when I happened into the warehouse proper. I promptly told him to shut up, to keep his opinions to himself or look for employment elsewhere. The look he gave me was one of pure hatred but he said nothing. Edward's brother, Edwin, was also in my employ but he was not the boisterous loud mouth his brother was. He was generally quiet and subdued but I had a feeling he was the more intelligent of the two."

At this point, Arthur Baines paused and looked at Pitt who had not said a word to interrupt his narrative. "I had not intended to be so wordy, Joshua, but this is the first time in years I have discussed my early life with anyone and I am remembering odd bits and pieces as I go along."

"It is an interesting tale, Arthur, please continue."

"Let me first recharge our glasses, or would you care for some tea, perhaps?"

"No, the whiskey is fine. I'll take a moment to recharge my pipe as well," said Pitt as he reached in his pocket for his tobacco pouch.

Baines returned to his chair, handed Pitt his glass, and resumed his narrative. "Several days later, at about midnight, a small group of hooded men gathered in front of Isaac Johnson's home and threw rocks through the windows. Johnson came out on the porch to defend his home and family and was promptly subdued, tied and dragged away, his wife screaming all the while. One of the hooded men hit her with a stave and left her senseless in the front yard. They found Isaac's body the following morning, hanging from a tree at the edge of a small patch of woods about a half mile from his home. I knew nothing of all this until I went to the warehouse the following morning when an under sheriff came to tell me. I was devastated and simply found it hard to believe. I went round to Isaac's home and proffered what comfort I could to his widow and placed one hundred dollars in her hands to take care of immediate needs. I later gave her a thousand more to help her and their son move back to her family in the Carolinas.

"I returned to the warehouse and gathered the men together. There was no need to tell them of Johnson's death. They already knew, but I wanted them to know how badly I felt about it. I also told them Emit Ferrall would be in charge of shipping temporarily. Emit, who was white, had been with me for about three years and had a good relationship with Isaac Johnson as his assistant. It was at this moment, Edward Becker made a loud comment to the effect that it was a "Goddam good thing they ain't goin' to be no nigger running this gang no more."

"I turned to him and in a level voice that surprised even me, told him he was fired. His brother, who was standing next to him started to say something and I told him he was fired as well and to collect whatever personal belongings they had in the warehouse and get out. They left, Edward screaming and calling me a bastard in addition to a few other choice names as they walked out. Twice, he repeated he was going to get me, that I'd pay dearly for firing him. Little did I know...

"Ten days later, at about two o'clock in the morning, my wife Alice woke me saying she thought she heard voices and noises on our verandah. I peered out the upstairs bedroom window just as a man wearing a hood ran across our front yard toward the house. I slipped on my robe, took a revolver from a dresser drawer, and went downstairs. I was moving to the front door when a brick came through the large sitting room window off to the left of the entrance hallway. In a rage, I simply lost my head, threw open the door, then charged onto the open verandah and slashed with the revolver at the first hooded figure I came to, striking him in the head. He went down. Whether it was surprise or shock at my actions, I know not, but the group backed up several paces, all except one. I reached out, grabbed his hood and tore it off. It was Edward Becker. He raised the axe handle he was carrying but I was quicker and struck him on the side of the head with my revolver. He went down as well, but my action had thrown me off balance and I fell to my knees. As I did, one of the men not three feet away pulled a pistol and fired twice. How he missed me, I'll never know, but both shots went wide of their mark. I raised my revolver and fired, hitting him center chest. He stumbled forward one step, then collapsed. The others, perhaps eight in all, turned and fled. They dashed across the yard and leapt over the picket fence that marked the front of our property. I got to my feet and saw that both men I had struck with my revolver were still unconscious. As I started to step forward to see to the man I had shot, I heard Alice call my name. I turned and went back to the front door. She was laying on the hallway floor just inside the door, blood coming from a bullet wound in her chest. A small pistol lay beside her. She had armed herself and come downstairs to help her husband defend their home. In minutes, she died in my arms."

Arthur Baines paused, drew in a ragged breath, took a sip of whiskey, and then continued. "By this time, the noise and confusion brought our gardener and general handyman who lived in rooms at the back of the house to my side. When he saw Alice, he let out a moan but I had the presence of mind to tell him to find some rope and bind the two men who lay unconscious outside. This he did, and then I sent him off to bring the sheriff. I stayed on the floor with my wife till neighbors arrived a few moments later."

"The remainder of that night is hazy, much like a thick London fog. The sheriff arrived and the man I shot and killed was unmasked. It was Edwin Becker, the quiet brother. He placed Edward Becker and the other man under arrest and asked only that I come to his office the following day to prefer charges. Good neighbors took charge of seeing to Alice and the family immediately next door took Mary Fiona home with them. I remember the next week only in bits and pieces: Charging the two men with attempted murder and complicity in murder, Alice's funeral, trying to explain to Mary Fiona, who was only three at the time, that her mother was gone. I felt as though everything in my life had been destroyed and had it not been for my daughter, I know not what I would have done.

Two months later, I gave testimony at the trial and ended by saying that my only regret was that I had not killed Edward Becker as well. This caused a stir among the jury as well as the spectators but the jury must have understood my anger and grief because they found both men guilty on both charges. Edward Becker was sentenced to twenty years penal servitude and the other man to twelve. A month after the trial, I sold the warehouses and my home, and returned to England with my daughter, first to London and within a year to this home in Kendal."

Baines rose, set his glass on the side table, walked to his desk, picked up an envelope and returned to Pitt. "This arrived eleven days ago, on Friday the 20th, and is the reason I have asked for your help."

Pitt removed the letter. It was hand written boldly in block letters, brief and unsigned.

YOU HAVE 26 DAYS TO PUT YOUR AFFAIRS IN ORDER - THE SAME NUMBER AS THE YEARS IN EDWIN'S SHORT LIFE.

Baines lit another cigar. "I am afraid there is not much to go on, Joshua, other than the threat, which must be from Edward Becker. If he served his full term, he would have been released last year but I have no way certain of knowing that."

Pitt tamped his pipe and relit it as he studied

the envelope. "It is postmarked Spitalfields, London, which may be useful. And I have contacts in the force who can confirm if Becker has been released. But tell me, why have you not gone to the police?"

"That was my first thought but after consideration, I rejected it for several reasons. I believed they might treat it as a prank, though they might think differently if I told them what I told you just now. Though the threat is here, it would of necessity involve the Criminal Investigation Division of Scotland Yard because the letter originated in London and communication between London and outlying jurisdictions is often not the best. In addition, I am sure they would wish to place the estate under some security measure, which if realized by Becker would only postpone any action he contemplates. Security would not only disrupt the running of the estate but if nothing overt occurred within the specified time, it would be withdrawn and leave the door open again for Becker. No, Joshua, I need this matter concluded unofficially."

"I am not an assassin, Arthur."

"I am not asking you to be. I am asking you to find this man and to determine if he can be bought, contingent upon his return to America. I would even agree to meet with him if he so desires."

Pitt finished his whiskey and took several long draws on his pipe before speaking. "Finding the man may be the easiest task. I think it highly unlikely, however, that he is going to give up a quest for revenge that has probably been his primary thought and motivation for twenty years.

I doubt money will deter him and meeting with him will simply provide him with an easy target. He may not care what happens to himself after he kills you. I truly believe calling in the police is your best alternative."

"I cannot do that. At least not now. I take it you are not willing to help?"

"I did not say that. I simply stated what I felt was the best course of action given the circumstance. Let us assume he started his countdown of days on the day he mailed this letter which in all likelihood was the eighteenth of March. If that is correct, then you have 13 days left after this one. If he added in delivery time, then you have an additional two days but I suspect not. He would assume you would count the days beginning with the *receipt* of this letter, a normal assumption on the part of most people, but that would also give him a two day edge. In effect, he would strike by his timetable, not yours.

"I had not thought of that."

"I suspect he did. He has had a lot of time to plan this. Also... I hesitate to alarm you unnecessarily but have you considered that your daughter might also be part of his revenge?"

"My God, no! I assumed... I simply assumed he was coming after me and if there was a threat to her, it would be small. Mary was only three years old at the time."

"And his brother was only 26. You took his brother. What would be more fitting than for him to kill your daughter, or worse?"

"What, then?"

"The first thing to do is find him, then negotiate

with him if possible. What are you willing to offer?"

"Twenty thousand pounds."

"A princely sum," said Pitt, knocking the dottle from his pipe. "And if he refuses?"

"Tell him I will meet with him here in Kendal to discuss it further."

Pitt smiled. "Will you kill him on sight? I will help you within the marginal bounds of legality but will not be party to premeditated murder, however rotten this man is. I will, however, endeavor to protect you in whatever way I can. I must see Hamish this evening while I am here and will leave on the morrow for London."

"But the time, man! Less than 15 days!"

"Time is on our side, not his. That is, as long as he keeps to the schedule he has given you and I suspect he will. I doubt it will take me three days to find him."

Baines looked at Pitt skeptically. "Three days?"

"Possibly less. I do have some respectable resources available to me."

Baines, smiled. "Ahhh... Your inspector friend in the Metropolitan Police of London."

Pitt smiled back. "I was thinking more in terms of a loose knit band of street Arabs I ran with occasionally, many years ago. I have used them to considerable success on several occasions, as have many other agents. I suspect they will get a line on your Mr. Becker in short order but what comes afterward may take some imagination. From your description, he is not a man who will scare easily, nor one who fears much, but all men fear something. I will think on it. Now, however,

I will take my leave and visit with Hamish who I believe also has a problem but not of the serious nature of yours."

"Will you be back here for dinner?"

"I think not. Hamish will have laid something on, I am sure, and I would not want to disappoint, but will return afterward. Before I go, however, I promised Fin I would meet his wife. He tells me she has improved."

"Markedly so, though I fear it may only be temporary. Fin is devoted to her. And by the by, Fin has proven to be a valuable asset. He is a Jack of all trades and a master of most, who takes to any new job in a trice."

"That is good to hear. He is a trusted friend. I will be off, then."

Fin's home was a stone cottage situated some one hundred yards from the main house and close to a stand of Red Elm that provided shade and shelter. He tapped lightly on the door which was opened almost immediately by Fin who stepped aside as he bade Pitt enter. Fin turned slightly to his left to introduce his wife who was standing at his side.

Alfred Finny's wife was a small woman but sturdy in appearance and looked to be in better health than Pitt had expected. She stretched out her hand and took his, pulling him slightly closer and planted a kiss on his cheek. "Tis pleased I am to meetcha sor. My Fin talks of ya most every day, bu' most all, I wanta tank ya for findin' us a place here... Tank ya from the bottom of me heart."

A bit embarrassed, Pitt mumbled something to the effect that Mr. Baines was pleased to have

Fin on his staff and that he was delighted to see Mrs. Finny looking so well.

"Aye, sor, I'm feeling much better," said she, lighting the gas ring under a tea kettle, "an' tha's also due to yur kindness. Would ya be havin' a cuppa?"

"Or somthin' a bit stronger," said Fin.

"Tea would be fine," said Pitt, pulling his pipe from his pocket as he sat down at the table. "Do you mind?" he said, indicating his pipe and looking at Mrs. Finny.

"Ach, no. Fin smokes a pipe in the evenings but I do wish he would find a bit sweeter tobacco. His is strong."

"Well, he is welcome to have some of mine. I get it from a shop in Oxford Street and it is a sweet smelling blend. Fin, you may have a chance to try some other tobaccos here in Kendal in a few weeks. Hamish MacLeod is taking over Welch's tobacco shop soon and has asked my advice about some of the tobaccos and pipes he should have in stock. I am going to see him later this evening."

Mrs. Finny poured tea for the two men and then put on her coat and shawl. "I will be goin' ta the main house for a few potatoes. Would ya care ta stay fur supper, Mr. Pitt?"

"Please call me Joshua, Mrs. Finny, or simply Pitt as most do. But thank you, no, I will not be able to stay. I promised Hamish I would call on him yet this evening."

Pitt took a sip of tea and then set the cup on the table. "Fin, I would like to ask about Edwin McNee's blackthorn, the one I received in the mail from you after McNee's death by misadventure while on a hunt. It appeared to have some blood and hair on it..."

Fin rose, walked to the sideboard and picked up an old pipe. When he sat again, he filled his pipe with some of Pitt's tobacco, taking his time as if thinking over what he wanted to say. "Well, sor, 'twere like this: Squire McNee were 'avin' trouble with the cinch on his saddle and turned back to the stables. We replaced the saddle and 'e were off again like a shot. Meself, not bein' sure what prompted me, ya understand, cut across a field in a direction that would 'ead 'im off. I weren't sure o' what I might do. I runs along a 'edgerow that were next to a stone keeper, ya see, an' I get ta 'edgerow break at the same time McNee is chargin' 'is 'orse ta jump the stone keeper. The 'orse sees me, 'alts an' rears, an' McNee's cudgel flies spinnin' straight up in the air whilst he goes 'ead an' arse over the 'orse, smashin' face first inta yon stone keeper. The Squire's cudgel come down, 'eavy end first, an' bashes 'im in the 'ead. But tweren't no never mind, I 'eard 'is neck snap like a pistol shot when 'e 'it the keeper. Were naught to be done, so I turns ta run back when I spies the cudgel and tinks ya might like ta have it. I gathers it an' sent it a few days later."

Pitt relit his pipe. "So, though you committed no overt act, you were in a sense responsible for McNee's death."

Fin smiled and set his pipe on the table. "Well, sor, ya might say it were shared by me'n the 'orse. Bu' I don' mind telling' ya, I 'ad it in me 'ead ta do some deed, bu' not certain what. Tha' squire were an bad un. 'E were not only guilty o' plottin' the death of yur intended, bu' treated all around 'im wors'n criminals at Newgate prison. Besides," he said, nodding toward the door, "I owed ya sor... for the missus."

"I know not what to say, Fin, other than thank you, and I am glad you were not directly involved. The next time you visit London, stop by my rooms. We will go to Simpson's for dinner."

"Aye, sor, I will do that."

They chatted for a few more minutes, Pitt asking how Fin's missus was getting along and was told she was much improved now that Mr. Baines doctor was looking after her. They finished their tea and Pitt took his leave. Baines had put a carriage and driver at his disposal so on his way to Hamish's cottage, he stopped by the post office to send a wire to Mrs. Keating to let her know he would be returning to London on the morrow.

Lowering clouds scudded across the sky and carried with them a chill with a promise of rain, a cold rain. The Lakeland area usually fared better than London with its weather but it seemed that London weather had followed Pitt north.

He had no sooner tapped on the door of Hamish's cottage than it was opened and as the last time he visited, he was greeted with a smile, a warm handshake, and an immediate offer of a wee dram, which Pitt accepted with alacrity. The cottage was quite old but with a cozy sitting room that sported a fireplace at one end glowing with embers of a coal fire. After Hamish filled and handed Pitt his glass, they settled in overstuffed chairs near the smoke darkened fireplace and lit their pipes.

Hamish looked at Pitt and smiled. "I thought

we might relax a bit laddie, afore we had supper. I hope you're hungry. I have prepared a dish you like: sweet-potato scones, baked ham, and cinnamon-honey cakes for dessert. And I laid in some Assam tea."

"I am hungry, Hamish, but tell me first of this pipe shop venture you have decided to take up. I admit I am a bit surprised. You seem to have quite the comfortable existence without engaging in the difficulties of shop keeping."

"Aye, lad, truth be known, it be a mite too comfortable, a tuppenny-ha'penny existence. Mayhap boring would be a better word. Managing a shop will give me some purpose, at least for a few years. As I said in my letter to you, Hiram Welch has been ill and the business has suffered because of it. Some days, the shop has simply remained closed. I have completed an inventory, but to my mind, the stocks seem haphazard at best, though I hesitated to say so aloud to Hiram. I would like to bring in some other brands of pipes and perhaps a wider selection of tobaccos but lack the experience to make the wisest choices. I thought you could help."

Pitt took a sip of tea, set the cup on a side table, drew a small leather bound notebook from his inner waistcoat pocket and drew out a slip of paper. "I gave it some thought after receiving your note and have written some suggestions for you. They are simply some things I might take into consideration were I to open a tobacco shop.

"The first item would be to review the inventory again to determine what stock had been on the shelves for six months or more without selling, or at least selling no more than twenty percent of inventory in that period. Whatever it is, you might want to consider reducing the price to ten percent over cost and get rid of it. If you want to try some different tobaccos, I have the address of the Tobacco Supply Syndicate, the Fairweather factory of Dundee and George Dobie and Sons of Perth, both in Scotland. You might want to buy some bulk tobaccos and blend your own that is unique to your shop.

"As regards pipes... well, you have to know your customer's wants as well as his purse. Makers such as GBD, Comoy's, and BBB offer good value for the money and I would recommend them. By the by, Comoy's opened a new pipe making shop in Newcastle Place, Clerkenwell, the year past and I have their address if you would care to write them. And of course, there is Peterson's of Dublin who offer fine, and I might add, very popular pipes at reasonable prices. A letter to Peterson's advising your position as the new shop owner will get you a catalog but I would suggest a couple days in London to visit the other pipe makers."

Hamish stared into the low fire for a moment. "I am certainly lacking in experience, lad, and thank you for your assistance. Do you suppose you could see your way clear to spend a couple weeks with me? Just to help me get my feet off the ground, so to speak."

Pitt picked up his glass and took a sip. "Fine whiskey, that. I fear I am engaged by Arthur Baines at the moment on a rather serious matter..." He paused, thinking. Being in Kendal for some other purpose than the Baines problem might be an advantage. "I have matters to take up for Mr. Baines in London but will be returning to Kendal in a few days, and would be happy to help you if time permits. Do you happen to know what pipes Mr. Welch has on hand at present?"

"I saw a few Peterson's and maybe three or four made in Scotland. Decent enough pipe they appeared to be, but not a brand I'm familiar with. Whyte, I think it were. Oh, and some clays also made in Scotland."

"Well, then, you may want to contact the landlords at the public houses and let them know you would be happy to provide clays if they don't already have a supplier. It is another line and not a particularly profitable one but it would provide you with a connection at the pubs and you could probably have the clay manufacturer put your shop's name on the pipes. Given that I have the time when I return to London, I will buy some mid grade pipes for you to open your shop with. Have you decided on a name for the shop? What is it called now?"

"Tis simply called Welch Tobacconist and I will surely change that but was thinking of something more general so that the name would not require change when I sell it in a few years. I will give it some thought and you might do the same." Hamish set his pipe on the table and stood. "Well, lad, to supper while 'tis still warm."

It was an enjoyable meal and they sat at the table afterward discussing a variety of topics including Pitt's recent loss of Eileen. No mention was made of the case Pitt was engaged in for Arthur Baines. It was not so much an ethical issue with Pitt as it was lack of meaningful information at this point. Hamish could certainly be trusted not to talk with anyone about it, but Pitt decided to wait till he returned from London when he hoped he could provide more particulars.

He returned late to the Baines household, had a pipe and a nightcap with Arthur and then turned in. Little more was said about the issue at hand, though Baines again expressed concern about his daughter. Pitt was also concerned but speculated that no attack would be made on Mary Fiona till the time specified by Becker was at hand. It was an assumption, of course, and one that could be proven wrong if something extraordinary occurred.

WEDNESDAY, 1 APRIL 1896

He rose early, completed his toilet and had tea alone on the glass enclosed portico adjacent to the diningroom. Baines had risen even earlier to tend to a livestock problem but Fin, who had been alerted by Baines, arrived with a carriage just as Pitt finished his tea and was lighting his morning pipe.

"Mornin' gov'nor. Me missus says to say g'bye but 'opes ta see ya soon."

"She will Fin, less than a week, perhaps only a few days, but the problem I've taken on for Mr. Baines requires me to return to London today. Remember what I said, that if you get to London, please let me know and we will have dinner."

"Tha' I will, sor, tha' I will."

The train trip back to London was uneventful. Pitt watched the countryside slip by, occasionally passing through areas of dense grey fog that collected on, then streaked down the carriage windows, leaving silver lines on the panes as if shedding tears. He arrived at Baker Street midday and as he entered the boardinghouse, could hear Mrs. Keating bustling in the kitchen, the clanging sound of pots and pans carrying to the hallway.

"I have returned, Mrs. Keating," he said loudly to overcome the noise from the kitchen.

She came into the hallway, the front of he apron spotted with flour, and her usual calm demeanor a bit out of kilter. "So I see, Mr. Pitt. Would you like some tea?"

"Yes, please, and would you send it up with the boy? I have an errand for him to run." He paused, then asked, "Are you having a problem in the kitchen?"

"I tripped on the cat and spilled half a large tin of flour on the table and it dusted some of the pans sitting there." She smiled. "I may as well make bread."

Pitt laughed as he started to climb the stairs to his rooms. "Well, if you do, send some up later with butter."

The houseboy arrived in his rooms a few minutes later with a pot of tea and some biscuits. Pitt handed him a few coppers and asked him to track down the leader of a band of street Arabs known as Gravel. Those urchins were able to go places and see things that an adult could not, and little or no attention was paid to them. Pitt needed them to locate Edward Becker.

It was an hour later that Mrs. Keating's houseboy reported back to say he had found Gravel and gave him the message from Pitt. But Gravel told the boy that due to being on a mission for another agent, he would send someone else along later that evening. Pitt preferred to talk to

Gravel because of his command over the ragged band but knew he could trust anyone sent.

It was an hour after dinner which included the fresh bread baked by Mrs. Keating, that there was a tap at Pitt's door. He was just lighting his pipe and around the stem he said, "Come in, 'tis open."

The door opened and in stepped a tall, gangly lad, almost as tall as Pitt but rail thin, appearing as all arms and legs. He was dressed in heavily soiled and overlarge tan coveralls held up by braces with metal fasteners. He stood, back to the doorway and looked around the room, his roving eye stopping at the pipes in the rack and several tobacco jars on the sideboard.

"Gravel said you needed someone for a job, Gov."

"I do. What is your name, lad?"

"Coffin."

Pitt put another match to his pipe. "First name or last?"

"Just Coffin, Gov."

"How old are you, Coffin?"

"Nigh on seventeen, sor."

"Well, you are a bit bigger and older than I expected but let me tell you what I need done and you tell me if you can manage it. If not, I will get someone else but in any case, will pay you for the trouble of coming here this evening. Fair?"

"Fair, Gov."

Pitt had notice Coffin's several glances at the tobacco jars and after telling him to close the door, asked if he had a pipe with him.

"Aye, sor, an old 'un," he said as he pulled an

old bent and much used briar from the large front pocket in his overalls.

"Help yourself to some tobacco and then take a seat over here near my desk." When Coffin was seated with his pipe alit, Pitt told him of wanting to find one Edward Becker, an American, and that he may be boarding in Spitalfields or nearby. He also provided as much of a description as had been given him by Arthur Baines but that description was years old. Pitt was emphatic that he only wanted to know Becker's whereabouts and habits, but that he did not want Becker to know he was being searched for or observed. He finished by asking Coffin if he thought he could do it.

"Aye, Gov, Spitalfields is a place I know well. If your bloke is there, I can find 'im. Give me two days. Me afternoons are not me own but mornings and evenings are."

"Alright." Pitt took some coins from his vest pocket. "Here are a few shillings to take care of any expenses. If you find him, there is a sovereign in it for you."

"I will find 'im, sor," said Coffin getting up from the chair and glancing at the sideboard. "You keep good tobacco, Gov."

Pitt rose, walked to the sideboard and put a couple ounces of Gawith's Virginia in an envelope and handed it to Coffin. As he did so, he asked, "Are you a gravedigger, Coffin"

"Aye, 'ow did ya guess?"

"Name, overalls, work in the afternoons only."

"Been at it a year. Pay is decent and afterward,

me time is me own. I will report back in two days at most, an' thankee for the tobak."

After Coffin left, Pitt changed into his heavy robe, poured himself a short whiskey, and lit a pipe. He stood at his sitting room window, staring out into the fine rain and fog that blurred the halo of gaslight from the lamp just a few feet from the boarding house front door. Apparently Baines is wealthier that I believed, he thought. Twenty thousand pounds, his offer to have Becker go away, was more than a princely sum, it was twenty years salary to a very well-to-do person. After all, the average family income was little less than £150 per year. Pitt smiled. He would keep that in mind when he presented Baines with his fee.

THURSDAY, 2 APRIL 1896

Pitt accomplished three important tasks the following day. First was a haircut and beard trim which was sorely overdue. Second, was a visit to both the BBB and Comoy's pipe shops where he selected and paid for a dozen pipes in standard shapes from each shop and had them sent to Hamish in Kendal.

His third stop was at Boss & Company, 73 St. James Street where he traded in his American Smith & Wesson revolver on a new Adams Mark II revolver in .450 calibre that fired the new Boxer centerfire smokeless cartridge. He was tempted to purchase a Webley Metropolitan Police model with 2 1/2 inch barrel but when shown an Adams with a 3 inch barrel, he was immediately taken with its comfortable hand-feel and lighter weight. The acquisition of the Adams would give him two extremely reliable revolvers of the same calibre: the Adams, and his trusted Webley & Scott with 4 1/2 inch barrel.

His late afternoon was spent in his rooms making a few entries in his account books and setting down some notes in his journal regarding the current Baines affair. Though he quite often joined the household in the dining room for dinner, he imposed on Mrs. Keating to have his evening meal in his rooms. He wanted to reflect on this rather singular affair of Arthur Baines' and would do so over a quiet meal and a pipe or two. Pitt was still uncomfortable with Baines' reluctance to involve the police though he had to admit his reasoning was well-founded. His concern for the safety of his daughter was understandable and it was true that even if the police provided some security, it would be withdrawn if no attempt on Baines' life were made in due time. And if Becker made no attempt as a result of police protection, it would leave the door open for some future attack just as Baines had said.

It had gone eight o'clock and Pitt was relaxing with pipe and whiskey in a wingback, his feet propped on the fender in front of a warm grate when there was a tap at his door. He opened it to find Coffin standing in the hallway, hat in hand.

"I found 'im, gov, just like you said, in Spitalfields."

"That was quick. Come in."

"Twernt 'ard. An American stands out kinda, in Spitalfields, an I 'ad help of another lad for 'alf the tobacco you give me."

"I will replace the tobacco it cost you. Come have a seat and tell me what you have learned."

"Well, sor, 'twas Baffle what found 'im - Baffle bein' the name of the other lad. The American 'as rooms over a public 'ouse called the Blue Duck on Chicksand Street just off Brick Lane. 'E's been there nigh onta two month an' there were a woman with 'im for a couple weeks or so but not now. An' 'e's the right un - name's Edward Becker. Word is, 'e spends 'is evenings at a corner table in the pub keepin' to 'isself. Quiet cove says the landlord; just sits watchin' the men what come in but talks to no one."

Pitt relit his pipe and passed his pouch to Coffin. "Was the woman an American?"

"The landlord said she might have come from up north, maybe Manchester, but 'e also said she had a funny way of saying things at times."

"In what way?"

"'E never said."

Pitt stood, walked to the sideboard, and picked up four ounces of Gawith's Flake tobacco wrapped in waxed paper. He returned to Coffin, handed him the tobacco, a sovereign, and two shillings.

"You have done well, Coffin, damned well, if I may say so. The two extra shillings are for Baffle. You will see that he gets them, please."

Coffin rose. "I will, sor, an' if you needs anything else, you can find me at East London cemetery or sometimes at Beckenham cemetery on Elmer's End Road."

"I will remember... and thank you again."

As Coffin closed the door, Pitt returned to his whiskey and pipe. He needed more information, some from America, and for that, he thought he could turn to Inspector MacLeish. The inspector would have to justify a cable to America some way but Pitt thought he could say that word of an American with a criminal record had come to his attention and he simply wanted additional information. Inspector MacLeish would find a way. And he would have to meet Becker to try to buy him off, a task he suspected would be fruitless. Early tomorrow evening would do, now that he knew where Becker hung his hat and tossed back a pint or two. He wondered about the woman as well, wondered if Becker had been keeping a whore, but whoever she was, she was no longer with him. "May or may not be important," he mumbled aloud, "but something to keep in mind."

FRIDAY, 3 APRIL 1896

He woke early, completed his toilet, and was sitting at his desk filling a pipe when Mrs. Keating came bustling through the door with a tray of tea and scones.

"'Tis a fine day, Mr. Pitt. Sunshine and comfortably cool. Too fine a day to be in the house so I will be going to market. Will you be here for supper?"

"No, I have an early evening appointment, so will be eating out, but thank you."

"Well, you will miss a fine roast but there will be enough for sandwiches on the morrow."

"I will plan on one for lunch, then. Would you send the houseboy up in about fifteen minutes? I will have a note to be taken to Inspector MacLeish."

As he ate, he composed the note to MacLeish. It was short, simply stating that he had reason to believe one Edward Becker, a convicted felon from Georgia, America, was in England and since Mr.

Becker might have some bearing on a case he was looking into, he was asking the inspector to query authorities in America about Mr. Becker. As an afterthought, he also asked for information about Becker's brother and brother's wife. Of course, he already knew Edwin Becker was dead but felt it most appropriate to ask for complete information. The houseboy arrived just as he finished the note and Pitt gave him a few coppers, but told the boy to leave the note with the duty sergeant if MacLeish was not in.

After finishing his breakfast, he put on his jacket and soft wool cap, slipped two pipes and a tobacco pouch in his pocket and left for Bradley Tobacco in Oxford Street. As Mrs. Keating had remarked earlier, it was a beautiful day and Hyde Park seemed to sparkle for the occasion. Some people wore smiles and one gentleman walking in the opposite direction was even whistling.

It was a short walk and when he entered the tobacco shop the bell Mick had installed above the door tinkled. Mick was standing near the rear of the shop measuring out some tobacco for a customer so Pitt stopped at the front case and looked at the pipes displayed there. Nothing piqued his interest so he filled and lit a pipe. Mick finished with his customer and came to the front of the shop.

"Is there any I can show you, Mr. Pitt?"

"I think not. Just some tobacco today. Four ounces of Gawith's Best Brown and two ounces of Arcadia should do it I think."

Mick moved to the rear of the shop and began measuring out the tobacco. "And how is the world treating you this fine day?"

"Fine, Mick, just fine. You're right, it is a beautiful day; one of the nicest in weeks. Tell me, do you negotiate individual contracts with pipe producers and tobacco blenders, or do you leave that to the syndicates?"

"Both. My tobacco, except for Gawith and Germain comes through the syndicate who act as distributors. That lowers the cost. Pipes are negotiated individually with producers with the exception of Peterson. The syndicate acts as the importer and single contact. Are you thinking of opening a shop?"

Pitt smiled. "No, but I have a close friend, a distant relative actually, in Kendal, who has taken over a shop and wants to upgrade his inventory and offer wider selections of both pipes and tobaccos. I thought I would gather some information for him and may even help out in the shop for a couple weeks. I've arranged for some pipes to be sent to him but I am vague on tobacco procurement. I just thought I would ask."

Mick laughed as he set the packets of tobacco on the counter. "Well, being in Kendal, at least he will not be competition. Profit on cigars, pipes and accessories is fair to good, but cigarettes, snuff, and pipe tobacco have a slightly thinner margin."

They talked for almost forty minutes, being interuppted several times by customers, and Pitt quickly realized that owning and running a shop was more involved than he had suspected. But it was also interesting and he found himself looking forward to acting as shop's assistant to Hamish in Kendal. If he liked it, maybe it was time for a change, if not in Kendal, perhaps somewhere else.

He paid for his tobacco, thanked Mick for the conversation, and walked back to his Baker Street flat. Upon entering the house, he asked Mrs. Keating for a pot of Assam tea and a pastry if she had any. She replied that she did and said she would bring them to his rooms in a few minutes.

True to her word just five minutes later, Mrs. Keating bustled through his sitting room door with a tray of tea and two apple tarts. She set the tray on his desk and as she turned toward the door, she said, "My houseboy said to tell you Inspector MacLeish would call on you in the morning if he is free."

"Thank you. And thank you for the tea and tarts." Pitt poured himself some tea and bit into one of the tarts. It was still warm and most certainly delicious, but his thoughts were on the later evening's task. There was always a chance of course, that Becker would not be at his regular haunt, the Blue Duck, but from what Coffin had said, Pitt thought it unlikely. Becker aparently liked his drink and had established a regular evening pattern that was unlikely to change. He felt certain he would find him there.

Several hours later, just as the gas lamps were being lit, Pitt emerged from his boarding house and walked to the end of the block to find a growler or hansom. Though he preferred a four wheel growler, the weather had remained decent and a hansom would do. A hansom it was. Pitt called out, "The Blue Duck on Chicksand Street," as he entered the cab and settled back in the seat.

He was wearing a soft wool cap, grey trousers and an old tweed jacket with a soft leather reinforced inner pocket that held his Adams revolver. Though he doubted he would have any need for it in a crowded public house, prudence dictated he carry it. He doubted Becker would cause any trouble that would deter him from his avowed appointment with Arthur Baines.

The Blue Duck was lit by a gas lamp about thirty feet off to the left of the front door which stood open, smoke from pipes and cigarettes rolling out into the street. Pitt paid the fare and went in, stopping just inside the door and off to one side. The room was crowded and loud but there was space at the bar and he headed in that direction. Several card games were in progress and as Pitt passed one table, a large bearded fellow dressed as a sailor and armed with a marlin spike was carving the initial R in the smooth oak tabletop. The barkeep, a short, fat, bald headed man of middle age, spotted him as he stood at the bar and gave him a hard look. Maybe he thought Pitt was a copper because of his dress but eventually asked what Pitt's pleasure would be.

As Pitt took an old battered Peterson pipe from his pocket that he had prudently filled before leaving his rooms, he replied that he would have a half pint of bitter. When it was poured, he lit his pipe and took a half turn toward the rear of the room. Sitting at a table alone was a man with receding sandy colored hair smoking a cigarette. He was clean shaven, broad shouldered, stocky build, and sat with one hand in his lap and the other with the cigarette, resting on the top of a pint of beer. He was simply watching the room, but not as if waiting on someone; just watching the people. It had to be Becker.

Pitt started across the room, pausing for a moment at the table where the sailor had just finished carving the R in the tabletop. Pit noticed other initials there as well and commented in passing.

"Adding your initial to the group?"

The sailor looked up and smiled. "Nay - Yon R stands for *Rank* ta describe the last whore I bedded. I keeps track on this table while in port."

Pitt raised his glass, laughed, and continued on to Becker's table. When he got there, he stopped directly in front of Becker, blocking his view of the room.

"Is your name Edward Becker?"

"Who's asking?"

Pitt pulled a chair from an empty neighboring table and sat down. "My name is Joshua Pitt, an enquiry agent, and I represent Mr. Arthur Baines."

Pitt expected Becker to be surprised but instead, he only smiled and said, "So the cowardly bastard sent a boy, did he? Thought I might shoot him on sight? If'n he showed hisself, I'd have half a mind to. Might be I could shoot you to send him a message. Course, he already has one message an' I figure that was enough."

Pitt slid his hand inside the flap of his jacket. "I have two things to say to you, Becker: The first is that if you try to shoot me, you will be dead before you can move back from the table. The second is that Mr. Baines would like to make you a financial offer to leave England and never return."

Becker's face registered obvious surprise, not at Pitt's threat, but at the offer from Baines. "What sort of financial offer?"

"Ten thousand pounds." Baines had told Pitt to offer twenty thousand but thought the lower amount might pique Becker's interest and he would ask for more.

Becker threw his cigarette on the floor and fished another from a pocket, lit it with a Vesta and took a drink of beer. He appeared to be thinking, maybe converting it to dollars. Pitt was wrong.

"So high and mighty Baines thinks he can buy his life and his... Buy his life for a bit of coin, does he? Not for fifty thousand, you hear me? Not for fifty thousand!" Edwards shifted in his chair. "I don't want his money!" he fairly shouted. "He can cram it up his ass for all I care. And something else, you pansy English bastard..." He paused as if choosing his words. "As much as I would like to personally even the score for my brother Edwin, it will not be by my hand that vengeance strikes. No sir, not by my hand..."

Pitt rose and looked down on the man. "Then I will tell you this, Becker. If harm comes to Mr. Baines or his daughter from any quarter, I hold you responsible and you will not leave this island alive." With that, Pitt turned and walked away.

The air outside the Blue Duck was cool and misty and clean by comparison. Pitt was angry. He would very much have liked Becker to have pulled a gun or at least made some overt act he could have responded to with force but knew intellectually it was best that it did not happen.

He had learned three crucial facts: money wasn't important to Becker, or at least not as important as revenge; whatever was planned included Baines' daughter; there was another person or persons involved. It was the last item that concerned him. Pitt was now certain there was someone else deeply committed to the murder of Baines and his daughter, as deeply committed as Becker, and whoever it was, was unknown. He would wire Baines in the morning to tell him he would be returning to Kendal in two days. Hopefully, Inspector MacLeish would have some information by then. At the corner of Chicksand and Brick Lane, he hailed a growler and told the driver to take him to his Baker Street digs. He had intended to get something to eat but twenty minutes in the Blue Duck had put paid to that. He had no appetite. Mayhap Mrs. Keating would provide a pot of tea and another tart.

SATURDAY, 4 APRIL 1896

The following morning after his usual Assam tea and scones, Pitt composed a very short message to be telegraphed to Arthur Baines:

NOT FOR ALL AT YOUR COMMAND. OTHER DEVELOPMENTS. WILL ARRIVE KENDAL TWO DAYS HENCE ON THE AFTERNOON TRAIN. ASK FIN TO MEET ME. PITT

Pitt rang for the houseboy as he reread his note and smiled. He wasn't one to laugh at another person's misery but this was obviously one dilemma that money would not solve. He handed the wire to the houseboy when he arrived, told him to take it immediately to the telegraph office, and gave him a few extra coppers for his trouble. He then went downstairs and told Mrs. Keating he would be leaving in two days for Kendal and would probably be gone at least a week, perhaps more. She did not need to save his newspapers but could keep them for herself to read. He had turned toward the stairs when the front door opened and Inspector MacLeish came in, doffed his hat, and said, "Good mornin' ma'am," to Mrs. Keating. She smiled and asked if he would like tea. He said he would and she replied she would bring some up to Pitt's rooms in a few minutes.

They settled themselves in the wingbacks located in front of the grate and Pitt indicated the jar of tobacco that sat on the small table between them.

"Help yourself, Angus, its some Arcadia I picked up yesterday."

"Thank ya, laddie, I think I will." The inspector fished in his pocket for a pipe, filled and then lit it. "I 'ave some information for ya, such as it is, but need a favor in return. The Chief Inspector is away for a few days, some conference in Glasgow, but on his return, 'e will want an explanation for a telegram to America. I dunae have one laddie."

"You can tell him a recently released convicted murderer has been reported in England and you suspect he may have followed someone here to do them harm. Tell him it was from an anonymous source. Except for the anonymous part, it may all be true. Tell the Chief Inspector you were simply being prudent and trying to stay a step ahead of any foreign criminal element. That should do it."

"Aye, it should, but can you tell me more, private like as it were."

"Not much, I fear. I am working on a case for a wealthy individual who lives in Kendal whose past was once intertwined with Edward Becker. Not in any criminal way, but as Becker's employer before Becker committed the crime that sent him to prison. The gentleman in Kendal received information Becker was in England and was concerned for the welfare of himself and his family, and so contacted me. I suggested, rather strongly I might add, that he seek assistance from the police but he has personal reasons not to. He is quite firm in that regard. At the moment, I am simply gathering information to determine why Mr. Becker is here in England. I suspect it is not a holiday."

MacLeish set his pipe on the table and took a folded, letter sized piece of paper from his inner coat pocket and handed it to Pitt. "Might it be a Mr. Arthur Baines of Kendal we are speaking of? Perhaps you had better read the reply. I had it typewritten from the telegram we received from the Savannah police. More readable."

Pitt glanced at MacLeish in surprise, then unfolded the paper, but before he could read it, Mrs. Keating bustled in with a small tray of tea and biscuits that she sat on the table between them. Pitt thanked her and turned to the paper again as the inspector poured tea for both of them.

Inspector MacLeish,

Regarding your enquiry as to the circumstances of Edward Becker. Edwin Becker, and Edwin's wife, we present the following:

Edward Becker returned to Savannah after serving almost a full sentence of twenty years for complicity in the murder of one Mrs. Arthur Baines.

Edward Becker's brother, Edwin, was killed at the time the murder took place. Edward Becker has not been seen in the Savannah area for several months and we assume he has moved to another city, though we have no information as to his exact whereabouts.

Edwin Becker's wife, nee Martha Fenton, emigrated from Sheffield England in 1866 at age 16 and married Edwin Becker two years later. She has lived quietly as a widow since his death. When Edward Becker was released from prison, he moved in with her as a border.

We have heard rumors, with no hard fact to substantiate them, that the relationship of Edward Becker and Mrs. Edwin Becker was more than of landlady to border. In addition, it should be noted that she sold her property and disappeared at the same as Edward Becker.

We assume you have reason for your query. If Edward Becker is in England, we would appreciate knowing, though he is wanted for no crime here.

Respectfully,
Earl Brown
Under Sheriff, Savannah

Pitt set the copy on the table and picked up his tea. "Your comment about Mr. Baines rather startled me Angus. I thought perhaps Scotland Yard had acquired some investigative methods I was unaware of but I see now how you easily arrived at the conclusion Arthur Baines was my client."

"This Edward Becker 'as made threats, then?"

"He has, but will deny it. And I daresay he might get away with it."

MacLeish set his teacup down, picked up he pipe and lit it. "If Becker confronted Mr. Baines personally, and there were witnesses..."

"But he did not, you see, at least not personally. Mr. Baines received a letter through the mail that threatened him and perhaps his daughter, though in regard to his daughter, it was vague. The letter was unsigned, in block letters - a copperplate hand - and probably copied, but contained enough information that Mr. Baines was convinced it was Edward Becker."

"Weel, 'twould appear there is enough to go on for the Yard to act in some capacity but since no crime 'as been committed as yet and Mr. Becker is 'ere legally, it would require a formal complaint from Mr. Baines for us to take up the matter. I assume Mr. Becker is in Kendal?"

Pitt warmed their tea. "He is not. He is in London and I have seen him. He shows no signs of leaving at present. Through me, Mr. Baines made him a financial offer to leave the country and never return, a substantial offer I might add, but Becker refused in no uncertain terms."

The inspector stood and put his pipe in his pocket. "I must be getting along. 'Twould be best if you could convince Mr. Baines to file a formal complaint. We could post a constable or two at 'is home in Kendal that might deter any action from Becker."

"I think he would prefer not to do that for reasons of his own but I shall tell him I spoke with you and you recommended it. I will be Kendal bound in two days and may be there a while, though at this point, I am not sure how long. If I can persuade Baines to follow your advice or if the situation warrants, I will send you a telegram. And thank you for your help and the information from America, Angus. I had no other resource."

After the inspector left, Pitt returned to his chair, propped his foot up on the fender and lit his pipe. Taking short puffs as was often his wont when thinking, he stared at the few lumps of coal cooling on the grate.

Without any proof, some things were simply intuitively obvious, a feeling deep in the bowels as it were. He was as now certain that Edward Becker spoke the truth when he said it would not be by his hand that harm would come to Baines as he was certain Mrs. Edwin Becker was in England. But where was she? It was most probably her who had been staying with Edward Becker at the Blue Duck Inn but had now been gone for two weeks or more. He had no description of her other than that she must be in her mid forties. He hesitated to ask MacLeish to send another telegram to America but it suddenly came to him there was another way. Coffin could get a description from the landlord at the Blue Duck. That would fit in easily with another task he had made up his mind to ask Coffin to perform.

On the spur of the moment, he decided to take himself out to an early dinner and walked downstairs to inform Mrs. Keating. While there, he gave instructions to the houseboy to find Coffin and ask him to come round to Pitt's rooms the following morning if possible but if not, to let Pitt know when he could be there.

Back in his rooms, he refreshed himself at the basin and debated where to go for dinner. He considered the restaurant in Grillon's hotel in Albemarle Street which was always excellent but also expensive. Not that he did not have the funds, he certainly did, but thought perhaps a less exclusive place might suit him better. He finally decided on Simpson's in the Strand. It was familiar and he was comfortable there.

Donning a soft cap and lightweight jacket, he stopped at the sidebar, chose two pipes and filled his tobacco pouch. On the way out the door, he selected his penang lawyer as his walking stick and was off. He hailed a hansom at the end of the block, sat back and lit a pipe, and watched ever changing London roll by as the cab bounced over the cobbles. Without knowing why, he always thought of London as a woman. A woman with everything a man could want. A woman who was a lady in public and a whore in bed. As a city, it ran the gamut between incredible beauty and indescribable degradation, and Pitt loved every facet of it. Though he thought of leaving from time to time, of making a life somewhere else, he was not convinced he could, or at least with any feeling of comfort. But things change... Things and people change.

At his instruction, the cab dropped him about a city block or a bit more from Simpson's and he leisurely strolled along, stopping occasionally to peer into a shop window. At a small antique shop, he stopped behind a rather tall young lady and was looking over her shoulder at a small pastoral painting when he noticed a scent of lilac. He had just made the connection when she turned and smiled.

"Why, Mr. Pitt, how have you been?"

"Elizabeth! Elizabeth Langston from St. Barts! I have been fine, thank you, fully recovered as you see. And you, have you been keeping busy at the hospital?"

"Of course. I am responsible for a first care ward at present but that will change soon. I will be leaving St. Barts within the week."

Pitt smiled. "It seems to be a season of change. I was on my way to have dinner at Simpson's. Would you care to join me?"

"Why yes, yes I would, thank you. You can fill me in on your latest adventures." She took his arm and they walked on toward the restaurant.

Pitt first met Elizabeth while working on a case given to him by another agent and he had recorded it in his ledger as being a successful and lucrative adventure, albeit one of theft and murder. It was in the midst of that case that Inspector MacLeish had been wounded, taken to St. Bartholomew hospital, and Pitt first encountered Miss Langston. There had been some duplicity on Pitt's part when he introduced himself as MacLeish's brother for fear that not being a member of the inspector's immediate family, he would not have been able to see him. Miss Langston had seen through it rather quickly and though she said she would not lie for him, a sort of conspiratorial and amicable relationship had arisen between them. This relationship deepened and became even more intimate when Pitt himself was wounded, shot in the right leg just eight inches above the knee. It was Elizabeth who made it her duty to nurse him back to health. They saw each other several of times afterward, once having lunch together but her duties as a nurse and his cases conspired to keep them apart. On one of those cases, he had met Eileen McNee and they planned to marry before she was so viciously murdered. That whole period in his life occasionally seemed as yesterday but just as often seemed as though it were a thousand years ago.

They ordered and while waiting for the wine, a fruity German Mosel Pitt favored with veal, he asked about a comment she made earlier. "So tell me, why are you leaving nursing?"

"Oh, I'm not abandoning nursing, it's my life's work. I love it. I'm simply leaving St. Bart's for a more responsible position at a new clinic opening in Kendal next week. I'll have four sisters who report to me and there will be two doctors on staff to begin with, but we expect it will grow larger in time." She saw the startled look on his face. "Is there something wrong?"

He laughed. "No, no, of course not. It is just that I am at present working on a case in Kendal that will take me there for about two weeks. It is nice to know you will be close by to nurse me back to health if I am shot again."

"You do not expect..."

He interrupted, "No, but it is quite a serious matter involving a threat to one of Kendal's more prominent families and could be a matter utmost moment for them as well as myself. But it is early days and may be resolved without violence. Much depends on being able to identify one of the threatening parties, a woman, as it happens." Pitt looked up as the waiter arrived with a chilled bottle of Mosel and continued, "Let us simply enjoy the evening and put puzzles and mayhem out of our heads for the present."

Dinner was a delight, as was the conversation, and Pitt found himself more relaxed than he had been in months. He truly enjoyed Elizabeth's company and found her to be, as he remembered her, an intellectual equal with a grand sense of humor and wit. He was very comfortable with Elizabeth, as she seemed to be with him, but at the same time, he felt guilty due to the tragic death of Eileen just several months past. Logically he knew that life goes on, that he might find someone else to share his days and nights with, but there you have it - an emotional tie still bound him to the past. Well, he would deal with it and in time, would overcome it.

After dinner they walked arm in arm, stopping to look in shop windows and occasionally to comment on clothes or books or jewelry. Pitt lit his pipe as they peered through the window of a closed bookstore.

She turned to him. "I love the aroma of a pipe and your tobacco smells delicious."

Pitt chuckled. "Delicious is not quite the term I would use but it is a heady aroma. The blend is Arcadia and I get it at Bradley's in Oxford Street. Interestingly enough, one of the things I will be doing part time in Kendal is clerking at a tobacco shop recently purchased by a relative of mine."

"Clerking! I cannot imagine!"

"It will explain my presence in the town and at the same time, permit me to become familiar with at least some of the people there. Folks seem to chat with their tobacconists in the same manner they might with publicans or barbers. Aside from that, I rather like the idea. I have given some thought to opening my own shop and this will be an opportunity to discover if I would like it."

She pulled him toward a small millinery shop. "Being a tobacconist would seem to me mundane compared to being an enquiry agent."

"Perhaps. But perhaps I am ready for mundane, at least for a while. As an enquiry agent, I have been successful, certainly financially, but recently, I have become tired of coming up against the seedier side of life and have been wishing for something more respectable and sedate. Not that I don't enjoy the oft confounding melting pot of the city, I do, but of late, it has had it's depressing moments." He paused, then continued, "And also of late, I have been thinking of how nice it would be to settle down and raise a family. With that in mind, I have been considering other lines of work."

He tamped and relit his pipe as they looked at the display of hats in the window. "I somehow have never thought of you as a hat person."

She laughed. "I am not. I prefer a scarf if I need one but I like to look at the styles." She hesitated a moment, then asked, "Do you have someone in mind you would like to raise a family with?" Then, as if regretting her question, "I apologize. It is none of my business, but oft times I am a bit forward and say aloud what I am thinking."

He smiled. "No, it is quite alright. And no, I am not courting anyone at present." They walked along is silence for a few moments before Pitt suggested a hansom to take her home.

"I fear I have offended you," she said quietly.

"In no way. But there is now a slight chill in the air and neither of us are dressed for cooler or even wet weather." He hesitated, then asked, "Would you be free tomorrow evening late, perhaps nine o'clock? I have business to attend to early in the evening and it would be after dinner hours, but would you like to have a pastry and coffee with me then?"

She smiled and squeezed his arm. "I am free and would be delighted to have pastry and coffee with you."

Pitt hailed a cab and within a few minutes they were at her apartment house in Bartholomew Close, just a few city blocks from St. Barts. Her apartment had its own private entrance, a convenience that allowed her to come and go at odd hours when she was needed at the hospital without disturbing other tenants.

Holding her arm, he walked her to the door. "Your company has made this a most enjoyable evening, Elizabeth, more enjoyable certainly, than dining alone as I had expected. I shall be here at nine tomorrow evening." He started to turn away when she put her hand on his arm.

"Joshua."

He turned to her and she leaned forward and kissed him lightly on the lips. "I have had a wonderful evening, the most enjoyable in a long time. Thank you."

Pitt was not so much surprised by the kiss as by a feeling akin to a hot flame that ran through his body from head to foot. Both kiss and feeling were unexpected and though certain he was blushing, he slipped his arm around her waist, pulled her to him and they kissed, this time both with a simmering passion. She pressed her lower body against him, so much so, he could feel the heat of her thighs pressed against his own, even through her skirt. When he released her, he smiled and said, "You're welcome," then turned to the waiting cab and continued, "Till tomorrow evening at nine." As he entered the hansom, he told the driver, "Baker Street," and settled back in the seat to consider this shocking, though pleasant, turn of events. His leaving, though it may have appeared abrupt, was not meant to be. He was simply at a loss for words.

Elizabeth Langston had rekindled feelings in him unfelt since he had last seen Eileen McNee, though surprisingly stronger. It left him somewhat in a state of confusion, a condition he was singularly uncomfortable with. And of course, his guilty feeling returned. He tapped the dottle out of his pipe, refilled and lit it, and sank back in the corner of the cab to think. By the time he reached his boarding house, he had no more clear measure of his feelings than when he left Elizabeth. Of one thing he was certain: Fate dealt unusual hands and at the most unpredictable times. Well, he would sleep on it. Perhaps by the morrow he would come to terms with the evenings events.

SUNDAY, 5 APRIL 1896

He woke to the bustling sound of Mrs. Keating as she set a tray of tea and scones on the desk in his sitting room as she did every morning, then proceeded to provide him with the local weather in a loud voice. He suspected the strength of her voice was more to assure he was awake than to announce the weather.

"Seven o'clock, Mr. Pitt. There's quite a chill this morning and a pea-souper of a fog. The gaslights are still lit."

Thank you, Mrs. Keating. Should I venture outside later, I will dress for it. By the by, did your houseboy manage to find Coffin yesterday?"

"He did, and said the lad you asked after would be here about nine this morning."

"Thank you again." He could hear her closing the door to his rooms as he put on his robe and slippers. As with almost every morning after completing his toilet and washing his face and hands, he went to the sidebar, selected and filled

58

a pipe with tobacco, then placed it on his desk as he sat down to break his fast. Unlike some he knew, he was not a heavy eater in the morning. He found a cup or two of strong Assam tea and a couple of scones were sufficient till lunch. And Mrs. Keating's scones were as good as any he'd ever had, being rich with cinnamon or ginger, though often with fruit when in season.

His thoughts turned almost immediately to Elizabeth. He would not go so far as to say he was smitten by last evening's events but was certainly captivated by it's rather romantic ending. There had been unexpected passion in that second kiss, and promise as well. Of that he was certain. Insofar as the guilt he felt about Eileen McNee, he had realized late last evening that it was more the betrayal of her memory than guilt. Once that was realized, it was simply a short step to the logical conclusion that it was just that, a memory, a loving relationship that was in his past; a loving relationship that would never be part of his future. He would always remember Eileen, remember they had planned a life together, but that dream of the future was gone, never to return. He had come to terms with it, reluctantly perhaps, but had reached some resolution nonetheless.

He finished his scones, refilled his cup and reached for his pipe. There were two items on his agenda today before he would see Elizabeth in the evening. First was his meeting with Coffin, and second was another go at Edward Becker in what he was certain was a fruitless attempt to convince him to leave England, his brother's wife in tow. He would offer Becker the full twenty thousand pounds proposed by Arthur Baines but was convinced it was a lost cause.

He had just finished dressing when there was a tap at his door. "Come in, 'tis open."

Coffin came in carrying a steaming cup obviously provided by Mrs. Keating. "Morning, gov. 'Tis a raw one this morning. Thick as soup and as 'ard to breathe."

"That is what Mrs. Keating was telling me earlier. I have another task for you, Coffin. Two, actually, but first, can you write?"

"Aye, of a fashion. Din't 'ave no formal schooling, did I?"

"Well, if need be, you can give the information I need to Mrs. Keating and she can pass it on to me. I will be leaving for Kendal in two days but will need to know immediately if Mr. Becker has quit his rooms at the Blue Duck. You will have to check daily to learn if he has. Have you ever sent a telegram?"

"No sor."

"Alright, in that case, come here and tell Mrs. Keating. She will wire me. But there is also information I need today. I need as complete and accurate description of the woman who was staying with Mr. Becker as you can get for me. I need her height, weight, age - anything about her you can learn. Can you do that?"

"Aye, sor, I will try."

"Fine. I will be away from here most of this evening so write it down and bring it to Mrs. Keating, or if you have a problem writing it, simply tell Mrs. Keating and she will write it for you. I am going to pay you well for your trouble, so do not fail me, Coffin."

"I will do my best, sor."

Pitt went to the sideboard, picked up a package of two ounces of Gawith tobacco he had wrapped earlier, and two pounds in coin. He was not sure what a grave digger earned but thought the two pounds might be equivalent to at least four week's wages or more. He returned to Coffin and handed him the money and tobacco.

Coffin smiled as he took both. "It be a generous cove you are, gov. Nowt beggarly about you - no slur intended.

Pitt smiled in return. "None taken, Coffin. If you provide the information I need, it will be worth it." He tapped him lightly on the shoulder. "Now, off with you."

Soon after Coffin left, Pitt donned a soft wool cap and mid-weight ulster, then slipped two pipes and his tobacco pouch in the coat pocket. He tucked his weighted blackthorn under his arm before picking up the tea tray to return to Mrs. Keating. As offensive as was the weather, he wanted to walk a bit and think, even if it was only to the outer circle of Regent's Park and back. He would liked to have walked to Hyde but if the fog was as thick as reported, he would spend all his effort finding his way instead of analyzing the Baines problem. And as much as he did not want to admit it, the possibility of keeping company, or an even more intimate relationship with Elizabeth was on his mind as well.

When he deposited the tea tray in the kitchen, he told Mrs. Keating that Coffin might leave a message for him later in the evening and if it was not a written one, to write it down just as he gave it. He also reminded her he would be leaving two days hence for Kendal. He added that Coffin again might have a message for him in his absence. If so, Mrs. Keating was to wire him immediately in care of the Arthur Baines residence, Kendal.

He left the boarding house and walked slowly toward the end of Baker Street where it dead ended into the park road The thick yellow-grey fog, heavy with moisture and smelling of sulfur from coal fires, had lifted some, but the few others out and about were shadowy forms at twenty feet or less. Something scurried across his path not more than six feet in front of him. A large rat followed by a second smaller one. He wasn't surprised. Rats seem to find their way, night or day, fog or no fog, and they plagued every part of the city from wharves to West End.

The criminal class often took advantage of the heavy fog to rob those worthy's who ventured out, either of necessity or unaware. Thugs usually worked in pairs, one in front and one in back, the one behind with a garrote. The garrote was usually made of hemp, not of wire. Wire could decapitate by accident or even intentionally, but the intent of the thug behind was simply to slip the loop over the head of the victim and hold him by force while the thief in front grabbed his purse or any other valuables. The garrote was a simple affair - a length of half inch hemp about three feet long with finger sized wooden blocks tied at each end for handles. The hemp was stiff enough that a crossed loop could be formed by a flick of the wrist. The loop would then be flipped over the head of the victim and both ends pulled, tightening the rope sharply around the victim's neck, rendering him helpless. The snatch and grab would be over in an instant and the hoodlums would be off, disappearing into the fog, their victim left half senseless and gasping for breath. Pitt was very much aware of this of course, hence the blackthorn walking stick weighted at both ends but lighter at the ferule.

As he walked along the lake path in Regent's Park, he put his mind to the Baines-Becker case at hand. He posed a scenario, a series of guesses, as you will. Some enquiry agents claimed they never guessed, but Pitt did. He found conjecture quite valuable and it had many times proven correct or at least led him in the right direction.

He imagined a chain of events beginning with Becker's release from prison. He did not know as certain, but assumed Becker was in touch with his deceased brother's wife while in prison and went immediately to her upon his release. That Baines returned to England soon after the trial would be common knowledge in Savannah and the pair would surely know that. They determined to revenge Edwin Becker's death and sold Mrs. Becker's house, the proceeds of the sale easily paying for their passage and expenses many times over. They arrived in London and began their search. With concerted effort, it wouldn't take an inordinate amount of time to learn the whereabouts of Baines and his daughter. A plan was laid and the threatening letter sent. Pitt even thought he knew the reason that lay behind the letter, a rather absurd thing to do on the surface because it alerted Baines.

First and foremost, Pitt believed, was to cause Baines turmoil and fear, which it had so admirably done. The pair wanted him to know that death would soon be knocking at his door. The second reason was a bit more obtuse, a blind meant to mislead, and it did. Not for one moment did Arthur Baines consider that someone else had joined Edward Becker in his act of revenge. But Mrs. Edwin Becker had, perhaps in more ways than one if the assumption of the Savannah police was correct. Whether Edward's relationship with his brother's widow, Martha Becker, was based on revenge, a serious relationship, or simply a sexual liaison mattered little. The result was the same.

Pitt was also convinced it was she who would carry out the act. That bit of guesswork was based solely on comments made by Becker at the Blue Duck, comments that could be construed as denial if, as he had been at the time, Pitt was unaware of Martha Baines presence in England. And it was Martha more than Edward who was predisposed to success. After all, she had been born and raised in the midlands of England, not emigrating to America until she was sixteen. A return to her native accent and earlier ways would be a simple task. She could blend in easily and she had disappeared from London. Pitt was certain she was in Kendal or nearby. But how she would attempt murder had to be more than guesswork. Bomb? Poison? The answers lay in Kendal and Pitt would be there on the morrow.

At half way around the park lake, the thick fog was beginning to tell on him and he turned to retrace his steps back to the boarding house and his rooms when he was passed by a shabby looking chap who glanced back at him as he walked by. At little more than twenty feet distance, at the point where the man was becoming a shadow in the fog, he slowed his pace to match Pitt's. It was then Pitt heard steps behind him. He was being set up for robbery, but whether the threat was by garrote, knife, or cosh, he had no way of knowing, though it made little difference. It would be the thug behind him who made the first move. Pitt slipped his pipe into his left coat pocket and moved his hand to a point about twelve inches down from the weighted, gnarled ball at the top of his blackthorn but made no attempt to turn around. The man behind moved rapidly closer.

It was garrote! An instant before the loop flipped over his head, Pitt moved the blackthorn vertically to a point four inches in front of his face catching the rope from the inside. He shoved his stick forcefully forward pulling the man behind almost up against him before the thug let go of the rope. Pitt spun round and slammed the weighted head of his stick into the bridge of the thug's nose. He heard bone crack like a pistol shot and the man went to his knees, covered his face with his hands as he screamed like a gutted hog. Pitt spun round to the other who was now no more than six feet away and armed with a large clasp knife. Instead of running, as the thief certainly expected him to do, Pitt took one long step forward and threw his left arm out wide. The man's eyes followed it as he suspected they would. Pitt swung his stick, ferrule end forward, caught the man flush on his left ear and watched as he dropped his knife and fell, holding the left side of his head, only half conscious and moaning.

Pitt turned back to the first man who was on all fours, blood streaming from his broken nose and smashed forehead, struggling to get up. Without saying a word, Pitt walked to the man and with both hands, swung his blackthorn, weighted top end down, and smashed it into the man's ribs. The thug let out a scream, not quite as loud as the first, and collapsed on the path. Pitt looked over the scene, smiled, and resumed his walk back to his rooms. In spite of the fog, it was a good day, he thought. He had sorted some things out, had a nice walk and a bit of exercise. He began to whistle in time with his stick tapping on the path.

After a delicious cherry tart with clotted cream that followed on the heels of a fine roast beef dinner, Pitt repaired to his rooms and lit an after dinner pipe. He must have complimented Mrs. Keating a half dozen times on the dinner and wondered afterward how he would fare if he ever left her boarding house. Not as well, he imagined.

Night had fallen and the fog that had plagued London was much the same as earlier in the day. He had promised Elizabeth he would be at her place about nine o'clock and determined the only way he could manage that was to have whatever cab he took from Baker Street wait for him while he visited the Blue Duck to see Becker. Well, a couple extra shillings would take care of that matter, he was sure.

He had just donned his coat and hat, and picked up his blackthorn, when there was a tap at the door. He opened it to find Coffin standing there with a grin on his face.

"Evening, gov," said Coffin, taking in Pitt's

coat and hat. "It ud be a poor night to be out in this swill, I can tell you."

"Bit of business to attend to. You have a description of the woman, then?"

"Aye. I started to tell your landlady but she said you were in so I come up. The woman you be askin' after is 'bout eight or nine stone, an' a shade over five feet, maybe two inches over. She 'as red-brown hair with a touch of grey, an' brown eyes." Coffin paused for a moment as if trying to think of anything else, then said, "Oh, an' the bloke I talked with at the Blue Duck also said she had a fair figure for a woman her age and some light freckles 'cross 'er nose an' cheeks. 'E thought she might be from up north somewhere but said at that, she still had a funny way of saying things at times."

"In what way?"

"Dint say, did 'e? Said 'e tried to give 'er a toss one evening but that Becker fellow put quits to it in a hurry."

"Thank you, Coffin. You have been a great help. Do not forget to let Mrs. Keating know if or when Becker gives up his room at the Blue Duck."

"I will, gov. G'night."

Leaving his boarding house to walk to the end of Baker Street for a cab, Pitt mulled over Coffin's description of Martha Becker. It was good, though somewhat general, except for one telling mark - the freckles. The freckles could be most helpful.

The Blue Duck was crowded but Pitt found a spot at the bar, ordered a half pint of porter and turned to survey the crowd. He located Becker, sitting at his corner table as usual and nursing a beer but also saw the sailor he'd seen on his last visit. The tar was busy carving another initial in his tabletop. Pitt picked up his beer, took from his pocket an old Peterson pipe he had filled on the way, and lit it before taking several steps to table to see what initial was being carved. He saw the original R for "Rank" followed by an O and could see the fellow was busy finishing up a B. The sailor looked up as Pitt approached and smiled. Pitt, smiled back, pointed with the stem of his pipe. "Planning to "ROB" someone?

"Nay, yon O is for the second bitch. She were Orfil."

Pitt did not tell him "awful" began with an A. "And the B?"

"That were the third. She were Beastly."

They both laughed. Pitt tamped and relit his pipe. "Mayhap you had best give up before you run out of words... or table."

"Aye. Well, I 'ave run out of time afore I 'ave run out of table or women. I ship out on the morrow. We sail early and I 'ave to be aboard this evening."

"Where bound?"

"Australia be our first port. God willin' I will be back in a year. One good thing 'bout Australia."

"And what is that?" asked Pitt.

"Better women."

They both laughed again and Pitt turned to walk to Becker's table.

Becker saw him approaching and smiled slightly, a sinister smile, thought Pitt, or an arrogant, knowing smile.

Becker stretched out a foot to the chair opposite

him at the table and pushed it out a ways. "Have a seat, errand boy."

All Pitt could think of was, "I'd like to get this bastard alone in a dark alley for ten minutes," but said nothing and remained standing.

Becker took a long pull at his beer. "You got somethin' ta say, errand boy, or you just goin' ta stand there like a goddam statue?"

"Mr. Baines would like to offer you twenty thousand pounds to leave England and never return."

There was a look of surprise on Becker's face and he paused for a moment before replying. "That is a tidy sum, boy, but I ain't goin' nowheres, least right away. You tell your boss when I go, it will be my own doins, not his. Now git the hell out o' here."

Pitt stared at Becker for a moment, then said, "I pity you."

"Why is that, sonny?"

"You do not have long to live... and neither does your brother's wife." And with that, leaving a shocked expression on Becker's face, Pitt turned and walked to the bar, set his barely touched glass of porter down, and started for the door. He paused at the well carved table and put his hand on the sailor's shoulder. "Good luck on your voyage."

"Thankee, lad. Mayhap I will see you in here next year."

"Mayhap," said Pitt with a smile. "What is your name?"

"Mike McCarthy, from Cork, but they call me Fish, cuz like me Da, I like to fish. An 'e be doin' a lot of that now. He quit the boats a year ago an' now lives 'long the coast near Dungarvan."

"They called your father Fish as well?"

"Aye, they did"

"I sailed a London-Dublin packet with him a couple years ago. When you see him or write, tell him Joshua Pitt said hello."

"I will do that, Mr. Pitt, an' be glad to."

They shook hands and Pitt left the Blue Duck. He found his waiting growler a few feet from the door under a dim, fog shrouded gaslight. He shouted Elizabeth's address to the driver, entered the cab and settled into the corner on the kerb side. Almost without thinking, he slipped his pipe from his pocket and lit it, then stared past the ribbon of smoke to the occasional sidewalk figures as they moved by.

The stinking fog wisped in and out of the cab windows around the half drawn canvas curtains as they rattled along the cobbles, bringing with it odors of rotten garbage, human excrement, coal fires, and other smells he could not name, nor would attempt to. London... a city of over four million souls with a huge percentage of unfortunates, many of whom turned to illegal means for a few coppers. He had recently read an article in the Times that claimed there were over sixty thousand prostitutes in the east end alone and almost as many scattered among the upper class communities. Though he loved what he called the "Magic of London," it was times like these and bastards like Becker that caused him to wonder why he stayed - caused him to question the sanity of his chosen profession. The police and even some private agents might be obsessed with crime and the criminal classes but Joshua Pitt was not. Oh, his occupation as an enquiry agent had provided variety, adventure, and as his bank account showed, a more than substantial income, but perhaps it was time for a change, if only a temporary one.

He pushed those thoughts back as they came to a stop in front of Elizabeth's boarding house. He paid the driver and pocketed his pipe which had gone out in any case, then made his way to her private entrance and tapped on the door. It opened almost immediately.

She stood with the light to her back, smiling at him, the glow catching the auburn highlights of her hair to the point that the light seemed to emanate from her head instead of the glowing gaslight behind her. She was wearing a simple emerald green shift that complimented her eyes and no jewelry but for a small gold link chain around her neck. All thought of the Baines case left Pitt.

She stepped forward, placed both hands on his shoulders and kissed him lightly on the cheek. "I thought perhaps you wouldn't come round with the fog as bad as it is. When I got off duty three hours ago, the hospital was kind enough to provide me with an escort equipped with a lamp, but even then we stumbled often on the pavement."

Pitt felt flustered and a bit uneasy, though he found it difficult to imagine why. He had been around women and had several relationships since he was sixteen, fleeting though most had been. He did manage a comment. "It is certainly a bad night and I am sorry for that. I had hoped we could step out for a sweet and tea but now I think it a bad idea."

As she took his coat, hat and stick, she said, "I thought the same, so I baked some apple tarts and have cream for them. Would you like coffee or tea?"

"Tea would be fine."

"I remember you like Assam but fear I have none. I do have a hearty Scottish blend that I like. Sit near the fire and warm yourself."

There were two chairs and table arranged in front of a standalone coal stove with glass front that sat near the wall to the right of the front door. Pitt moved to one of the chairs while taking in the room. The kitchen area was a deep alcove off the sitting room, while a short hallway with one door left and another right, led to what he assumed was a bedroom and a private lavatory. A very nice arrangement, he thought. Comfortable and cozy.

Elizabeth put the kettle on, then came into the room to sit in the other chair. "I noticed the weight of your blackthorn when I set it against the coat tree. It must weigh a pound."

"A bit less than two. I had it drilled and leaded at both ends though the pommel end is heavier. It has protected me on more than one occasion."

"Tell me, Joshua, if you change your livelihood to something more sedate, will you not miss the challenge and adventure that seem to have been constant companions for you?"

"I have thought of that. A commonplace life can become mundane rather quickly I suppose, for someone who has been exposed to danger on occasion. There are some who seem to thrive on it and I must admit, it has moments..." He paused and lit his pipe. "But you must remember that many of my cases are mundane. Divorce, embezzlement, errant husbands or wives, and other quite ordinary cases take up more than half of my time. Admittedly, I have been compensated handsomely in some instances. Just the other evening, I was thinking I could spend a year or two traveling around the world if I choose, but then what? Back to being an enquiry agent again? I think not. On the other hand, I am certainly in a position to purchase an agreeable home, have it tastefully fitted out, and buy into a small business or start my own. And as I said last evening, I would like to have a family - a son perhaps, to hunt and fish with."

"And smoke a pipe with? What if you have daughters?"

"Well, a daughter can hunt and fish." He paused, then laughed. "I am not so sure about the pipe smoking, though."

The kettle was boiling. She got up, went to the kitchen and returned shortly with a tray laden with teapot, mugs, apple tarts in bowls, spoons, and cream. She set it on the table between them. "Nothing fancy, I fear, but there are more tarts if you want another."

"I think one will be sufficient. I added a few pounds while visiting Ireland several weeks ago."

She poured tea and then some cream over the tarts. "You carry it well, but then, I have not seen you for months till yesterday."

"And a dog."

Elizabeth put some milk in her tea. "What about a dog?"

"I was thinking that along with children, I would like to have a dog. Maybe a herding dog as they have in the borderlands. As a young lad, I always wanted a dog but we never lived in a place suitable for one. Mayhap I will raise sheep."

She laughed. "I simply can not bring up the image of you as a shepherd."

Small talk. They both felt that magnetic excitement that was drawing them together but neither were ready to move in that direction. Pitt felt it, wanted to set aside the small talk, the tea, the tarts, and take her in his arms - crush her to him, make love. But propriety also made for confusion. If a long term relationship or a lasting one was in the making, it might be best to go slowly. He had not countenanced her strong and forward nature, however.

She took a sip of tea and looked at him over the cup. "The night is a bad one, Joshua, and it will be all but impossible to find a cab. I think you should stay the night."

He looked around the room. "I would agree, but the chairs do not look all that comfortable."

"I was not thinking of chairs."

Pitt paused for a sip of tea. "Neither does the floor."

"Nor was I thinking of the floor. I have a large double bed and I want you to share it with me. I want you to love me, Joshua."

He was not shocked, surprised perhaps, but not shocked. After all, it was what he wanted as well. But other than some tart making a pitch on the street, he had never encountered a professional, upper class woman who would make so bold as Elizabeth had just done. She was strong, intelligent, well educated; a woman who could match his own wit and will with repartee, conversation, and undoubtedly passion.

"Elizabeth..."

She stopped him by reaching across the table and putting her finger to his lips. "Joshua, I was attracted to you the first time I saw you. That was when inspector MacLeish was wounded and you came to St. Barts posing as his brother." She smiled at the thought, as he did, then went on. "When you returned, wounded, just a day or so later and I took care of you, I knew I was in love with you. Though we met for tea several times and I had hopes of something more, you had cases that kept you very busy for months, and some that took you out of London. I had lost hope. Then yesterday, fate, or providence, or chance, put us together in the Strand and I am determined to not let this moment pass."

Gently, he stretched out his hand and placed it against her cheek. "Nor am I Elizabeth, nor am I. There is something I want to share with you, however, and it should not, will not, change anything. I promise."

She sat, listening intently, as he told her of his relationship with Eileen McNee, her death, and his revenge that followed. He told her of his trip to Ireland to be with friends in an attempt to put it all behind him, an effort that was only partially successful until he met her and had such a delightful dinner the previous evening. He realized then that they were in so many ways, compatible - in so many ways, kindred spirits. If nothing else, their kiss had confirmed it, even though it left him in a state of confusion for the day afterward. He smiled. "I have to admit I was still in somewhat of a confused state when I came to your door this evening."

"I noticed," she said, laughing.

He laughed as well but then became more serious. "I want you to know two things of importance. The first is something I had to come to terms with and have. I can not be in love with a ghost. The second is that you need not feel you have to compete with a ghost."

"That is all I need to know, Joshua. Nothing more." She paused a moment, then stood. "Would you like more tea or another tart?"

"No, I think not, but thank you. If you do not mind, I think I'll light my pipe."

"Is it the same tobacco you smoked last evening? I liked that."

"Yes. Arcadia. It is one of my favorites though I occasionally smoke a different blend, but none so strong as black shag. The reek and odor of black shag has been known to drive even smokers from a room and that includes myself.

Elizabeth returned from taking the plates and teapot to the kitchen and stood next to his chair. She stared down at him with the hint of a smile and what appeared to him as a bit of a blush on her cheeks.

"I bathed after coming home from the hospital," she said. I am afraid I do not have any men's things such as razor or shave soap but if you would like a bath or to freshen up, you should be able to make do with what is in the lavatory. I will turn down the lights and wait for you in the bedroom."

"Since I only shave my neck below my beard

a couple times a week, I have no need of a razor tonight." Pitt laid his pipe on the table, got to his feet and reached out his hand for hers. He pulled her close and kissed her gently, very gently, on the lips. "But thank you, I would like to freshen up a bit. I won't be long."

She had taken care to put clean linens on the bed in hopes of this moment but could hardly believe it was really happening. She was thrilled, excited, and at the same time, embarrassed and apprehensive. She had little experience in matters of romance, having only once given herself to a young soldier she was fond of. But that had been almost three years ago and the young man soon received word that his regiment was to ship to India in a matter of days. She never heard from him nor saw him again.

She slipped out of her shift, removed her undergarments and laid them on a chair in the corner, then climbed into bed. It was a tall bed with teak headboard, down mattress, and covered in a pale blue feather-down comforter of European style. It had been her one extravagance since entering the nursing profession as a sister, having convinced herself that with all the hours she worked, she should have a good night's sleep. She shook her head slightly as she lay down and her auburn hair spread out on the pillow. Almost as an afterthought, she pulled the comforter up to cover her breasts.

Barefoot and wearing only his trousers but carrying his other clothes, Pitt came through the door, stopped, and simply looked at Elizabeth. "My God, but you are beautiful."

She held out her arms to him. "Come to me, Joshua, and love me."

He closed the door, turned down the gaslight, let his trousers slip to the floor. She turned toward him, lifted the edge of the comforter and he slipped into bed, nuzzling her neck as he did so. He kissed her and she responded with passion, pressing her body against his and then gave a shiver of pleasure as he moved his lips from her neck to the hard nipples of her breasts. Slowly, the intensity of their lovemaking increased. Then he was on top of her. He slipped his hand under her buttocks lifting her and she rose to him, bending her knees and raising her legs as he entered her. They moved slowly at first, then as passion took them, faster, thrusting wildly and pressing against each other as they became one. They reached orgasm together and as they did, she opened her eyes wide and let out a moan that matched his own and the sound was anything but stifled. They lay quietly for a moment, neither saying a word, and then Pitt chuckled.

"Are you laughing at me?" she asked quietly.

He rolled slightly to one side but still with his arm around her and his face close to hers. "No, of course not, he whispered. It is just that I'm very happy... But the thought did occur to me that we may have awakened other tenants in the house."

She laughed. "Or perhaps any in neighboring houses?"

They both laughed together and then Pitt turned to slip out of bed.

She turned to her side. "Are you leaving me so soon?"

He stepped to the gaslight, turned it up slightly

and picked up his jacket. "I am just getting my pipe. A few puffs seem appropriate."

"Has anyone ever mentioned you have a small arse?"

He half turned, match poised over the bowl of his pipe. "I have to admit, you are the first. And is not *arse* a bit risqué for a young, upstanding lady?"

"You forget I'm a nursing sister. I certainly have heard every slang, curse, and swearword under the sun and some of the combinations are quite imaginative." She paused as he came and sat on the edge of the bed, pulling the cover over his legs. "Joshua, I am deeply in love with you. I simply thought it before but now I know it as if it were etched in my soul. I never want to be with anyone else."

"Nor I, Elizabeth, my darling Bess. I knew that somehow before I even entered this room, before our lovemaking. There is a rightness to it, a rightness to us. Whether it is fate or the hand of Providence, I know not, but I do know it is what ought to be. I desire no other woman to share my life."

She put her hand on his leg. "Then I shall consider us engaged." But as if a thought had suddenly occurred to her, she hesitated. "Oh, I am rushing things as usual. Forgive me."

"There is nothing to forgive. We re engaged if we say we are engaged but I have no ring to give you. But wait a moment..." He took several short puffs on his pipe and then blew a smoke ring. "Put your finger through that."

By the time the ring drifted to Elizabeth, it

was several inches across and she put her hand through it to the wrist. "There, I'm committed."

He smiled. "I should say so. And so am I, ring or no." He set his pipe on the bedside table, walked to the gaslight and turned it down before he got back in bed. He slipped his arm around her waist and whispered, "Now where did we leave off, hmmm?"

MONDAY, 6 APRIL 1896

Morning came soon enough and Pitt woke feeling warm and comfortable, knowing immediately where he was and remembering the passion of the night before. "I could get used to this bed," he mumbled as he reached out his hand for Elizabeth. She was not abed but he then realized he could smell coffee. She must be in the kitchen. He rose, slipped on his trousers, and padded silently through the sitting room, following the aroma of coffee which grew stronger with each step.

Elizabeth turned toward the small table, coffee pot in hand, and saw him leaning against the edge of the kitchen archway, arms folded across his chest and smile on his face. "You are as pretty in the morning as you are at night."

She set the pot on the table and came to him, wrapped both her arms around his waist and nestled her head on his shoulder. "Oh Joshua, I

81

feel so complete, so whole. It is as if I have waited all my life for you to make it so. I do love you."

"I love you too, Bess, very much. Do you mind if I call you Bess? I never thought to ask but I do like it."

"My father called me Bess and I like the name, so you have my permission." She stepped back and smiled. "I barely remember my mother. She died when I was but three years old, though I do remember she called me Elizabeth, so you have a choice. I hope you do not mind but I made coffee this morning. I have a French press that I rarely use but coffee seemed appropriate to match the weather which is still foul. Not as bad as last night but soupy and grey."

"I usually have Assam tea, as you know, but coffee is fine. Better in the morning than at night when it would keep me bright eyed till the wee hours. I see you are dressed in blue and wearing your apron. Do you have to go to St. Barts this morning?"

"I can think of something else I would rather do, but yes, I have to be at my post at seven o'clock. Would you like to walk with me? It is but ten minutes."

"Yes, I'd like that. Pour me a cup and I'll be back in a few minutes."

Toilet complete and dressed, he came into the kitchen and sat at the table. "I suspect I'll have a busy day today because I will be leaving on the morrow for Kendal. Would you like to have dinner this evening? ...And an overnight guest?"

"I would love both. Would you like me to fix dinner? My shift at the hospital will end at four and I can cook, truly."

He reached across the table and took her hand. "I would like that very much. I expect it will be about eight o'clock before I return but will be earlier if I am able."

She laughed.

"Something I said?" he asked, releasing her hand and picking up his cup.

"No, but I was thinking how hard it will be for me to concentrate on my duties today, remembering last night and looking forward to this evening."

He smiled in return. "You are not the only one who will experience that same predicament today."

They were a short distance from the hospital, making their way through the sooty grey of a cold and damp London morning, Elizabeth's arm linked in his, when an empty growler came past and Pitt hailed it. "We will ride in comparative comfort the rest of the way," he said as they climbed in, "and I will then have a cab to take me to Baker Street." After arriving at a side entrance to the hospital, he helped her out of the cab and they embraced briefly, Pitt kissing her lightly on the lips.

"Till this evening, then."

"Till this evening, Joshua."

His usual and automatic lighting of a pipe while riding in a cab was all but forgotten as he contemplated the recent happenings in his life. A few short days ago, he was mourning the loss of Eileen, albeit to a lesser degree than a month previous, and yet he now found himself engaged to Elizabeth. He regretted nothing, certainly not the passionate relationship he had with Bess, and was convinced he loved her deeply. She was bright, warm, loving, and above all else, an intellectual and conversational equal he could confide in. What had him shaking his head was the lightning speed with which it had all happened. He smiled thinking back to the previous evening and the vision of Elizabeth taking command of the situation and clearly expressing what she wanted. One could never accuse her of being introverted.

The thought of her having his children pleased him immensely and he was as certain she would make as wonderful a mother as she would a wife. His responsibility would be to provide safe and comfortable surroundings for a family and though it could be found in London, he preferred that it not be. And yet, he wondered why he would prefer someplace else. He was quite comfortable in London and was sure that Elizabeth, experienced a nursing sister that she was, could easily find a position at St. Barts or another hospital instead of her assignment to Kendal. Well, he would give it some thought and talk it over with her.

As his cab entered Baker Street from Marylebone, his thoughts turned to Edward Becker. It was the practice of one agent friend of his to try to determine the intelligence and cunning of an opponent early in the game and it was good advice that Pitt followed. In Becker's case, he felt the man was lacking on both counts but did not underestimate his determination. Then again, it might be the other player who was the most determined. Perhaps it would be worth one more try to convince Becker that money in the pocket was worth more than a bullet in the body. Though

Becker had turned down the second and more generous offer, Pitt sensed some hesitation when he did so. And then another thought occurred to him… perhaps it wasn't Edward Becker who was the driving force behind the planned attempt on Baines' life. It was entirely possible that it was Martha Becker, Edwin's widow, who had hatched the plot and Edward who was simply the vehicle. The more he thought of it, the more it made sense. It was conjecture, of course, and with no proof, but it felt right and he had learned long ago not to disregard feelings and intuition. Ah yes, another conversation with Edward was in order and this time, with a twist.

He alighted from the growler, paid the driver, and entered his rooming house to find Mrs. Keating waxing the banister at the foot of the stairs.

"Ah, Mr. Pitt, you must have had a long night, as you look tired. I hope it was successful."

He smiled. "Yes, a long night, and I do believe it was worth it though I'm afraid it will be the same tonight. I shall be leaving early evening and do not expect to return before setting off for Kendal early tomorrow morning. Since I plan to be there for an undetermined period, I will wire and let you know before I return."

Mrs. Keating set her cleaning rag on top of the tin of wax. "Your inspector friend was by and left a message for you. He said it was important he talk with you and would return again early in the afternoon, perhaps two o'clock."

"Thank you. I'll make a point of being here."

"Would you care for a pot of tea?"

"I would love one, and a scone if you have one."

"No scones, but an apricot tart."

"That will do nicely. Thank you. I'll be in my rooms."

He took two pipes and his tobacco pouch from his pocket, laid them on the sideboard and then hung up his coat and hat. The thought occurred to him that after more than two years of living on Baker Street, he would miss these rooms and Mrs. Keating if he were to move, whether that move were to be to some other part of the city or to a place other than London. Speculation at this point, he thought, pure speculation. Something to consider in the future but not now. He went to the fireplace, raked the ashes to one side and by the time Mrs. Keating came bustling in with refreshments on a tray, he had a decent fire going and the chill that had greeted him when he came in was gone.

After tea and tart, he checked his desk clock and determined he had enough time before the inspector arrived to visit his barber for a trim and to have his neck shaved below his beard. What little shaving he did need was usually done by himself but it was always a pleasure to have a barber do the job. Aside from that, it was clearing outside with sunshine breaking through scattered clouds and the walk would do him good. He filled and lit a pipe, pocketed his tobacco pouch and after donning a light tweed coat, was down the stairs and out the door in less than two minutes.

Several hours later, neatly trimmed and his

neck smoothly shaved, he was sitting at his desk when there was a tap at his door.

"Come in, Angus."

Inspector MacLeish, derby crowned and with ulster over his arm came in to take a chair across the desk from Pitt. "How did you know it was me at your door?"

Pitt laughed. "I could reply that I could tell by your step, but in truth, I was not expecting anyone else."

MacLeish smiled and nodded in response. "Weel now, it could have been Mrs. Keating, but then, you have said several times she never knocks so 'twere a good guess." He reached for the glass tobacco jar on the desk to fill his pipe.

Pit smiled. "Help yourself, Mac."

"Thankee, lad, I will."

"It is good you have come this afternoon," said Pitt, "because I am leaving early next morning for Kendal."

After putting a second match to his pipe, the inspector leaned back in his chair and pushed the derby back from his forehead. "Kendal and Baines is why I am here, lad. I wired back to the Savannah police that we are certain that Edward Becker is in London and has been accompanied by a woman, though we could not confirm that woman as Martha Becker. It was the reply we received that I though might interest you. It seems Martha Becker had a cousin, son of her father's sister, who emigrated to America with them. He would be about two years older than Martha and his name is Jonathon Foyle but he fancies Jack. The police telegram went on to say he roomed with Martha on several occasions after her husband died, once during a rough spot in his marriage. His wife died four years ago of consumption. But here be the interesting part: He also disappeared at the same time as his cousin Martha and Edward Becker. If she is in England, then it is not a stretch that he most likely is too. The Savannah report went on to say the man was a troublesome sort who had taken to drink at an early age and was arrested several times for brawling but had been charged with no serious crimes. It seems you may have three players in this mess, lad, and I am bound to say it might be best if you could convince Mr. Baines to involve the local police."

"I am in agreement with you, Mac, but I have doubts that Mr. Baines will be. I will do my best however. This new information puts a different light on the case and may carry enough weight to change his mind. He does not know yet about Martha Becker and the addition of her cousin in the mix may tip the scales our way." Pitt paused a moment to tap the dottle from his pipe and refill it. "Would it be possible, if I cannot convince Baines, that you could find a way to come to Kendal in a few days? Unofficially of course. If my calculations are correct, the Beckers will attempt something according to their schedule. They have made no indication of change and given their vengeful nature, I suspect they would. They want to worry Baines and keep him guessing."

"I might be able to arrange a few days holiday but I can hardly tread on another copper's patch, officially or unofficially, without raising an eyebrow or two. I am not known by sight in Kendal, however, so it might be done if I had some out of the way place to stay."

"I am certain Mr. Baines would have no objection to you staying at his estate and in fact, would welcome it. Do you have a description of Jack Foyle?"

"Not as yet but I wired to the Savannah police this morning for one. I expect it may be waiting for me at the Yard when I return. If so, I'll send it by messenger. If not, I will send it on to Baines' residence when I get it."

They chatted about a few other things and though Pitt considered mentioning his serious relationship with Elizabeth, he held off saying anything for the time being. Time enough for that if MacLeish came to Kendal or even later. It did occur to him that since Elizabeth's parents were now deceased, she might consider the good inspector as the chap to give her away at the wedding. Lord! The wedding! He did not even want to think about it at present.

After MacLeish took his leave, Pitt busied himself with packing. He took only a couple changes of clothes, knowing that if he needed more he could purchase it in Kendal. After placing three pipes and a package of tobacco in his Gladstone, he wrapped his Adams revolver, cleaning equipment, and a box of ammunition in oilcloth and placed them in the bottom of his bag as well. Though it probably was not necessary, he hoped he might have an opportunity to practice with the gun on Baines' estate. As confident as he was in the firearm and as comfortable as it felt in the hand, firing a dozen rounds or so with it would reinforce the feeling. Because he planned to go to the Blue Duck to see Becker that evening, he toyed with the idea of carrying it but felt it unnecessary in the crowded public house. If Becker had the murder of Baines foremost in his mind, as previous meetings indicated, he was unlikely to start something that might end with his arrest.

At about six o'clock, he parted the curtains of his window overlooking Baker Street and peered out. The lamplighter was making his rounds but there appeared to be no fog. Pitt donned his ulster and soft cap, then put two pipes and a full tobacco pouch in his coat pocket. He picked up his weighted blackthorn, tucked it under his arm and was bending to pick up his bag when there was a tap at his door. He opened it to find Mrs. Keating's houseboy there with an envelope that he handed to Pitt. Pitt thanked him, set down his bag and opened the envelope. It was the description of Jack Foyle from inspector MacLeish and read:

From Savannah police. Foyle is of average build and 155 pounds - 'twould be about 11 stone - Faint birthmark about the size of a fingernail high on left cheek. Red hair and balding. Walks with a limp when tired due to breaking a leg several years ago after falling down a flight of stairs while drunk. If I am successful at getting leave in a few days, I will wire you in care of Arthur Baines. MacLeish

Well now, thought Pitt, it was a good description and Jack Foyle should be easy to recognize if he was in the Kendal area, though he suspected he was not, at least not just yet. Then again, they had no proof he was in England but for the circumstances that led Pitt to believe he might be. At least he had the advantage of being able to watch for him.

He hired a four-wheeler at the end of Baker Street, gave instructions to take him to the Blue Duck and told the driver he would have to wait but would make it worth his while. He tucked his bag under the ledge of the seat and sat back in the corner to light his pipe.

Shops were closing and people were bustling to hearth and home along the gas lit streets. If what he had read in a recent Times article was correct, the city fathers were pressing to change the gas lights to electric ones but only on certain thoroughfares for now. Perhaps one day, all of London would be lit by electricity. Some of the streets in newer parts of the city were being covered with macadam and though it meant a smoother ride, Pitt suspected he would miss the clatter and sway of a growler as it made its way over the cobbles. Victoria, God willing, would celebrate her diamond jubilee the following year and continue to provide the stability needed for the empire to prosper. Times were changing.

The carriage pulled to the kerb in front of the Blue Duck and Pitt alighted, pausing only for a moment to tell the driver again that he should only be a few minutes and to wait.

The Blue Duck was crowded and as he had in the past, he went to the bar to order a half pint of bitter before relighting his pipe, then turned to see if Edward Becker was at his usual table. He was but something was amiss. His face looked as though he had run headlong into a wall. Pitt turned to the publican.

"Did the gentleman at the corner table have an accident?"

"You mean the American chap?"

"Yes. When I last saw him, his face was in better condition than tonight."

"Condition be a good word. 'E's ugly by any lights. 'E picked a fight with a sailor who sat at yon table. Might 'ave been brewing for some time. The sailor made an offer to the American's lady friend some days afore she left. She nor the American took to it well. Then again, tha' sailor were makin' offers to every woman who walked through the side door. The sailor were just leavin' and the American came cross the room an' grabbed him by the jacket. Well, the sailor took one step back pulling the American forward an' at the same time threw a straight punch that broke the American's nose. Heard it break from the end of the bar. As the American staggered backwards, the sailor followed through with another punch that caught the bloke square on his left eye and knocked 'im cold. It were ten minutes afor he woke."

Thinking a reply was needed, Pitt said, "If it was the sailor I am thinking of, the American was a fool to pick a fight with him. He must outweigh the American by two stone or more and is a head taller."

"Yeah, tha' be the right one."

Pitt picked up his bitter, walked to Becker's table and sat down across from him without saying a word.

Becker raised his head. "Here to make another offer?"

"As a matter of fact, I am. Leave England before

someone else finishes the job that sailor started...
permanently."

"That bastid blind-sided me, but I'll get him."

"That is not what I have heard, which makes
you a liar among other things, but no matter. The
sailor shipped out this morning for Australia so
if you want a chance to get even, you have a long
trip in front of you." Joshua paused but Becker
said nothing so he went on. "I want to be certain
you have not changed your mind about accepting
Mr. Baines generous offer. I will not come back to
this tavern again to ask."

Becker raised his head and Pitt winced.
He could see just how much damage had been
done by just two punches from the sailor, Fish
McCarthy. Becker opened his mouth to speak,
closed it, then said, "I tol you onct I will take no
amount of money. Now leave me be!"

Pitt got up from his chair leaving his beer
on the table and turned toward the door. As he
did, he heard Becker mumble, "Ain't my decision
anyway." Pitt almost turned to question whose
decision it was but already knew. It was Martha
Becker's. The only question in his mind was
whether Edward had conveyed the offer to Martha
or not but suspected he would have done so and
it was turned down.

His cab was waiting and as he entered, he
gave Elizabeth's address to the driver and then
settled into the far corner, fishing for the filled
pipe in his pocket as he did so. He lit the pipe and
mulled the situation over. They now had three
prospective murderers to contend with: Martha
and Edward Becker, and Martha's cousin, Jack
Foyle. Of the three, he was convinced Martha was

the most dedicated and dangerous. Edward was known on sight, at least to Pitt, but they only had descriptions of the other two, albeit decent ones. If MacLeish could come to Kendal, it would be a distinct advantage but it might not be enough. Convinced he would have to enlist some help, with or without Baines permission, he made a decision to tell the entire story to Hamish and Fin, two friends he knew he could count on.

The growler pulled up in front of Elizabeth's flat and Pitt dismounted, his bag in hand, pausing for a moment to give the driver a generous tip in addition to the fare. As he started for the rooming house door, it opened, and Elizabeth, framed in the doorway with light from behind shining round her, reminded him of angels often seen topping trees at Christmas time. She had changed from the blue dress and white apron of St. Barts and was wearing a floor length robe of deep burgundy.

He paused in front of her. "You look like an angel."

"I am *your* angel."

"That you are, lass, that you are." He dropped his bag, took her in his arms and kissed her."

She smiled. "Mayhap we should go inside. Passers by will think they are seeing a performance at the Holborn music hall... or worse."

He laughed. "Ah, but the streets are practically deserted."

"Yes, but the nearby houses are not."

They went inside and he set his bag by the coat stand and removed his ulster and hat. "Something smells delicious."

"Potatoes with onions and spices are simmering and I stopped by the butcher's to buy some veal cutlets. I also managed to pick up some Assam tea. Would you like a cuppa?"

"I would love it. Strong, please."

"I assumed that. Have a seat by the fire and light your pipe. It will be ready in a couple minutes."

He fished a pipe and tobacco pouch from his coat pocket and filled the pipe as he made his way to one of the wingbacks by the fireplace. As he propped one foot on the fender and lit his pipe, he made a decision to tell Elizabeth of the Baines case he was working on. There was some danger involved and she deserved to know.

Over dinner, dessert, and a second pipe afterwards in front of the fireplace, he did just that. She listened intently, asking only a few questions and finishing with a comment Pitt tended to agree with: "Baines may be a successful land owner and wealthy, but he is a fool if he does not involve Scotland Yard or the Kendal Constabulary. I will not say you are out of your depth, Joshua, because you obviously are not, but you are certainly outnumbered."

"I agree, but I do have two things in my favor. The first is that we have a given date when they intend to strike and I do not believe they will stray from that unless something extraordinary occurs. The second is that I can depend on Hamish, and particularly on Fin to provide some assistance. That tends to even the odds somewhat. More helpful still, is if Inspector MacLeish can see his way clear to come to Kendal for a few days. I will not rule Arthur Baines out but will not count on him for assistance. His nerves are strained to the breaking point now and in any case, his concerns should be directed toward his daughter."

She smiled. "There is one consolation."

"And what, pray tell, is that?'

"I will be there to patch you up if you get hurt."

He chuckled. "Aye lassie, there is that, but I have no plans of being hurt." He paused, then asked, "Are you scheduled for St. Barts in the morning?"

"I am. It is my last day and then I will follow you to Kendal two days hence."

"In that case, should we not be abed soon?"

"Mr. Pitt! Is that what is called an ulterior motive?"

"In truth... yes."

She stood. "In that case, the loo is yours and I shall meet you in the bedroom. The kitchen can wait till morning because I can not."

Again they made love, but this time, slower, more deliberately and with equal or greater passion. Afterwards, as they were laying side by side she turned to him and asked, "Would you like your pipe?"

"I think not, Bess. I am out of breath," and they both laughed.

TUESDAY, 7 APRIL 1896

The following morning the air was crisp and cold but without fog, just a light haze from the coal fires in almost every home. Pitt walked Elizabeth to the hospital and then flagged down a hansom to take him to Euston station for his trip to Oxenholme, there to transfer to a local train to Kendal. The wait was generally less than an hour but enough time for a cuppa and scone or biscuit while waiting. He supposed he could get a carriage to Kendal, it was but a couple miles, but he had made arrangements for Fin to meet him at Kendal station. Aside from that, he simply enjoyed trains. In a sense, trains were an adventure with ever changing scenery passing by the window. And if one became drowsy, the click-clack of the wheels on the track could lull one to sleep.

When he stepped from the train at Oxenholme, he was surprised to see Fin come toward him from near the station master's office. They shook hands and before Pitt could ask, Fin told him Mr.

Baines was anxious to see him and thought it would save time were Pitt to be met at the transfer station instead of Kendal.

"Tis a matter of some urgency, sor, an' if you will ride atop with me, I will tell you what I know."

Fin led the way to the carriage that was sitting beside the station office and Pitt threw his bag inside before climbing up top. He had barely settled in the seat when Fin whipped up the horses and they were off with a lurch.

"So tell me, Fin, what is the urgency?"

"Tis the young mistress, sor, she went missing last evening."

"What do you mean, went missing? She disappeared from her home?"

"No sor, not from the manor. She went into town mid afternoon to do some shopping an' after was to dine with a lady friend and family. I were to pick 'er up at nine o'clock but when I arrived, 'er lady friend told me Miss Mary had not been there for dinner and they had not seen her."

"She might have had an accident."

"I went into the town center but it were fair deserted save for the pubs an' I knew she would not be found in one. Tinkin' as you did, sor, I looked in at the clinic as well but they 'ad not seen 'er. I told all this to Mr. Baines when I returned but he insisted I take 'im back into town to search and we did so till after midnight. She were not to be found. Mr. Baines is at wits end, sor. He were ravin' this mornin' about killing some bloody sod if it were the last thing he did."

"I can imagine. Fin, I am going to need your help. There is not enough time to explain now, as we are getting close to the Baines residence, but after I have seen Mr. Baines I will explain matters to you ."

"Right, sor. Anythin' ya need, ya can count on ole Fin."

As they pulled up to the front of the manor, the front door opened and Arthur Baines rushed down the portico steps to the carriage. He was pale, disheveled, obviously shaken, and looked as though he had not slept the night.

"Mary Fiona has gone missing, Pitt! Missing since last evening!"

"So I was told by Fin. Let me get my bag. Fin, remain here for a moment."

Pitt removed his bag from the carriage and turned to Baines. "What errands had Mary gone into town for?"

"Errands? Goddam it, what does that matter? Someone has taken her!"

"It matters a great deal, Arthur. Now, calm down and tell me."

Baines took a deep breath and wiped his face with his hands. "She was to go to the McCain Millinery for a hat and then to the Smythe and Poole Emporium to look at cloth for a dress. Then she was to have dinner with the Yost family. They have a daughter the same age as Mary."

Pitt set his bag on the step. "Did you hear that, Fin?"

"Aye, I did."

"I want you to go into town and question the staff at both the millinery shop and the emporium. Find out when Mary arrived, when she left, and if she spoke to or met anyone at the shops. Tell them you are inquiring for Mr. Baines and nothing more. After you have done so, and I repeat, *after*, you will then go to the town hall and ask the chief Constable to come to the Baines residence on a matter of some urgency. He can ride back with you if he chooses, or take his own coach, but do not volunteer any information."

"Right, sor, I'm off."

Pitt turned to Baines. "I assume you have not notified the police."

"I am not sure, Joshua, that this is a matter..."

"It is without question a police matter, Arthur. It may not be necessary to go into detail about the reasons we believe are behind Mary's abduction, for that surely is what it is, but we need the assistance of the police to look for her. I have not been idle in London and have much to tell you. Your study?"

"Yes, yes of course."

Pitt had to admit to himself that he had been wrong. He had assumed any threat to Baines' daughter would come at the same time as to Baines himself. Mary Fiona's abduction may have only been opportunity presenting itself but nonetheless, it is something he should have considered. He should have warned Baines not to let Mary go anywhere unescorted. Pitt followed Baines into his home as Fin drove off in the direction of Kendal. When they entered the study, Baines went directly to the sideboard, poured two whiskies, handed one to Pitt and then settled into a chair in front of his desk. He motioned Pitt to the other but Pitt remained standing.

Pitt took a sip of whiskey and then set the glass on Baines' desk. "I have deferred to your wishes thus far regarding direct police involvement, but the disappearance of your daughter Mary Fiona, in addition to other developments that came to light while I was in London, make it imperative we call them in"

Baines leaned forward in his chair. "What other developments?"

"Edward Becker is not in England alone. It appears that he has been accompanied by his brother's widow, Martha, and her cousin, one Jonathon Foyle, known as Jack. I suspect, though I am not certain, that it is Martha who is the force behind the plot against you and not Edward."

Pitt went on to tell Baines what he had learned while in London and that of necessity, he had shared the information with Inspector MacLeish of Scotland Yard, though the inspector's involvement was unofficial. He finished by saying, "I believe we must now make it an official enquiry. What began as a threat by what we supposed was one individual, has now been compounded by the addition of two others and the disappearance of your daughter, who I am sure was kidnapped."

Baines finished his drink and stood to get another.

Pitt moved in front of him. "I am not a man to tell another what he should do in his own home, but I think you have had quite enough whiskey for the moment, Arthur. Fin will be returning soon with the constable and you look quite the mess. Best you take a few moments and have a bit of a wash and change clothes."

Baines scowled, then set his glass on the desk. "You are right of course, Joshua. Thank you." He paused, then went on. "Do you think they have harmed Mary? I couldn't bear it if anything happened to her." He appeared to be on the verge of tears.

"In this instance, I am guessing, something that is an anathema to the police and some other agents, but I have given it some thought and do not believe they will harm her, at least not yet. Bluntly, Arthur, Mary Fiona is of no value to them if she is dead. Alive, she is a bargaining chip, though we know not yet in what way. Guessing again, I suspect she will be used in some manner to lure you to a place where they can kill both of you. I am hoping we can remove that advantage before it comes to that."

"How...?

"We will talk of it later. First, you need to take care of yourself."

Pitt set his whiskey on the desk, fished in his pocket for his pipe and tobacco pouch and then sat in the chair Baines had indicated when they first came in. As he filled and lit his pipe, he was thinking how fortunate they would be if they only had some of his London street urchins in Kendal to scour the back streets, public houses and byways of Kendal for some sign of Mary Fiona or Jack Foyle. Then again, the chief constable would know well the town, and they did have Hamish and Fin who could provide some assistance, though Hamish would be of little help during the hours his shop was open.

There was always the possibility Baines' daughter was not in Kendal but Pitt somehow doubted they would spirit her out of the city. The towns within a short distance had an even smaller population than Kendal and whoever took her might be easily noticed. In addition, the Baines family was well known and Pitt suspected the daughter would be recognized on sight. No, it might be a guess, but he felt certain Mary Fiona was being held somewhere in Kendal.

In a few moments time, Baines returned to the room looking refreshed and dressed in tan flannel trousers, white shirt open at the collar, and black tweed coat. Ignoring his drink, he sat down behind his desk. "I've asked my cook to prepare a pot of coffee. Would you like some or should I have her prepare tea as well?"

"Coffee will be fine, thank you. Tell me, Arthur, how many really trusted men do you have on your staff? Old hands, if you will.?

"Three... four including Fin. And two women, Elsa our cook and Hannah who is in charge of the house staff. Both women have been with us for years."

"I think we can keep the women out of it for the time being. That is not a slight to the women for they are often equal to, or in some cases, superior to men when it comes to detecting, but in this instance, I think not. I believe the man we seek is a heavy drinker and we can't have the ladies walking unattended into a public house."

"You have a plan, then?"

"Not actually a plan, but more in the way of disjointed conjecture and suspicion. Pitt then proceeded to outline what he thought they must do and how he felt they must go about it. "My first thought was to raise a hue and cry publicly. Involve the newspapers in addition to openly bringing the police in. That would seem to be the natural reaction to a kidnapping. Doing so, however, would put them more on their guard than they already are. In addition, it would be a departure from your original response of not informing the authorities and instead, seeking the assistance of myself, a private agent. And if my reading of him is correct, Edward Becker at least, believes he is more than a match for me. I must say that it is no more than conjecture on my part, but I suspect Jack Foyle and Martha Becker are not living together in the same household but that wherever Jack is, is where we will find Mary. By tomorrow, with no general outcry, he will have relaxed a bit and unless he has a plentiful supply of drink on hand and no desire for company, he will visit one or more of the public houses. I am sure such a visit would be contrary to Martha's orders but the desire for drink will most probably drive Foyle to leave Mary, if only for a short time. If we can find the public house he most frequents, we may be able to identify the neighborhood he is living in and from that, the house where he boards."

"But there must be a dozen pubs in the town and though Jake, my man in charge of the stables, might occasionally frequent a local, none of the others do. If they begin asking questions, is it not possible that Foyle might be alerted?"

"Possible..." Pitt paused to relight his pipe. "But I think we might depend on Hamish to help us. He has lived here for years and though not a frequenter of public houses, he certainly knows many of the landlords or barkeeps. In addition, he has now established himself as a tobacconist and some of those employed by the pubs may be his customers. I will see him this evening."

"And when we discover where she is being held?"

"Then we will act, but only as an adjunct to the police. Kidnapping is a capital offense and they will take the lead, or at least seem to. I am hoping Inspector MacLeish will be able to come to Kendal on the morrow. While I am thinking of it, do you have a man who can ride into town and send a telegram for me?"

"Yes, certainly. Jake Jacobs should be in the stables. I'll have him saddle a horse and come to the house."

As Baines left for the stables, Pitt took a piece of paper from the table and with Baines' pen wrote a short telegram to MacLeish that read:

Angus. New developments. Urgent. Now a police matter. Come at once and wire arrival time Kendal. Pitt

That should get him here quickly, he thought. He did not want to mention Mary Fiona or kidnapping, feeling certain the telegrapher would soon spread the word, though their ethics code did not permit it. Some things slip out in conversation over a pint and Pitt was not going to take a chance.

Baines was back in a few minutes with Jake, a sparse man with shock of grey hair and deep furrows on his face that told of a life out of doors. Lean and sinewy, he was of indeterminate age though certainly over sixty, but with the look of a man who could hold his own against adversity.

After being introduced, Pitt addressed him directly. "Jake, I want you to take this telegram

into the post office and send it to Inspector Angus
MacLeish of Scotland Yard. Tell the telegrapher we
expect a reply and want it delivered immediately
to Joshua Pitt at Mr. Baines residence. I expect it
will come yet this evening."

"Right you are, sir. I'll leave immediately."

Pitt set his pipe down and took up his drink.
"Well, we have set some things in motion at any
rate, but there is much yet to do. Fin should be
back with the hour, bringing with him your local
constable."

"You have done more in 30 minutes, Joshua,
than I have done in a day. I thank you for that. I
am afraid I rather went to pieces."

"Understandable under the circumstances but
you seem to have pulled yourself together well.
If my calculations are correct, we have but six
days before the deadline given you in the letter.
But that is a vague number, is it not? If we count
the day the threat was mailed, then we have four
days. If they allowed two days for delivery, we
have eight. What it means is we should be fully
prepared for any eventuality in four days and for
several days afterward. But for the moment, your
daughter is our immediate concern.

We will need our wits about us to rescue Mary
and to meet our three adversaries head on, though
if we can succeed in taking Jack Foyle, we will
only have two to face. And while I am thinking of
it, I expect a telegram from London if and when
Edward Becker departs the public house where
he has been lodging. I have asked that it be sent
here but I intend to take up residence Riverside
hotel in town so it will be incumbent upon you to

relay it to me as soon as you receive it. If I am not there, I will leave word where I can be found."

"Why not stay here?"

"Because I believe the answers to some of our questions can be found more readily in town and I can respond more rapidly there, though I may be wrong. In addition, I hope to spend some time in Hamish's shop. It is possible I can get a line of Jack Foyle and Martha Becker there, though if they are not users of tobacco, then perhaps not. In any case, I prefer to be at the center of things and it seems the center is in town for the time being. If you don't mind, I would ask that Inspector MacLeish stay here. I think it would add a margin of safety and when Mary Fiona returns, some piece of mind. Do you not agree?"

"Of course, of course. You are in charge, Joshua, and I will follow whatever direction you set out. But above all else, we must get Mary back safely."

At that moment a middle aged maid came through the study door bearing a tray with coffee, biscuits and jam. She set it on a table at the far end of the room near the book shelves. "Will there be anything else, sir?"

Without turning, Baines replied, "No, Maggie, that will be all. Thank you." She curtsied, turned, and went out the door, closing it as she did.

For the next hour over coffee and biscuits, Pitt again, at Baines' request, retold what had transpired in London. He had just finished saying he was convinced that although Edward Becker was part of the plot, it was Martha Becker who was the driving force behind it when the door to the study opened and Fin entered with the chief constable.

Introductions were made and when Fin indicated he would wait outside, Pitt told him to stay and have a seat by the desk, saying it would save him from repeating the background of the matter later.

Constable Ian Royce was a stocky, middle aged man of average height and clean shaven except for side whiskers showing flecks of grey as did his dark brown hair. When he spoke, there was a hint of a burr, perhaps Yorkshire, but many years ago. "Your man Fin, told me it was a matter of urgency, Mr. Baines, but no more."

"It is, Mr. Royce. Please take a seat and Mr. Pitt will explain it. Would you care for tea, or do you prefer coffee?"

"Tea would be excellent, sir. Thank you."

Baines rang for tea and then took a seat at the side of the desk while Pitt remained standing behind it.

"Mr. Baines daughter, Mary Fiona, has been kidnapped," said Pitt, after setting his cup on the desk.

When Constable Royce gave a start and opened his mouth to speak, Pitt motioned him to silence in addition to saying that questions could come later. He then proceeded to relate the account of Baines time in America and all that had happened there, pausing only when a maid brought a fresh pot of tea. He then told of the threatening letter Baines received and of his own failed attempt in London to convince Edward Becker it would be in his best interests to return to America. He added they were convinced the disappearance of Baines' daughter was connected and most probably a kidnapping; a plot hatched on the spur of the moment, as it were, when the opportunity unexpectedly presented itself. For that reason, Pitt believed Mary Fiona was most probably still in Kendal but they knew not where.

Constable Royce appeared thoughtful for a moment, then said, "I could bring in several extra constables from neighboring villages and search door to door..."

"You could," interrupted Pitt, "but I think we should be more subtle, more circumspect. Raising a public hue and cry might eventually find Mary but I am convinced it would also put her in grave danger. We believe it is the intention of the Beckers to murder Mr. Baines as well as his daughter and pressure brought to bear as the result of a search such as you suggest could prompt them to do away with the young lady immediately. I believe Jack Foyle may be the one who is holding Mary. He is the weak member of this murderous group and unpredictable if rattled." He turned to Fin.

"Did you learn anything useful before you saw the constable, Fin?"

"Aye, sor, I did tha'. I went first to the Smythe and Poole Emporium, bu' no one there remembers seeing the young lady. At McCain Millinery, she be remembered well due to 'er being a regular customer. Miss Baines tried on several 'ats and when she 'ad made 'er choice, decided to wear it. Mrs. McCain said she noticed that when the young lady left the shop, she were greeted by a man and woman, an' she seemed to know the woman. From their gestures, the conversation was about the 'at Miss Mary 'ad just purchased.

They then walked together down the street away from Town Center. It were after talking wi' Mrs. McCain tha' I drove to get Constable Royce."

"You say she seemed to know the woman," said Pitt.

"Aye, Tha' be wot Mrs. McCain said."

"That could mean nothing or it could mean everything." Pitt paused in thought for a moment, then turned toward Constable Royce. "I have taken the liberty of contacting Inspector MacLeish of Scotland Yard and expect he will arrive tomorrow. It was he who wired Savannah police and provided crucial information about Martha Edwards and Jack Foyle."

"There will be no objection from me," responded Royce. "First, because we can use all the assistance we can get, and second because I know of Inspector MacLeish. I had the pleasure of working with the inspector several years ago on a case of larceny that involved a local bank. Though I never met the inspector, it was him who acted very quickly on information we provided and made the arrest of the felon in London. His presence would be very welcome."

Pitt tamped and relit his pipe. "How many constables do you have at your direction, Mr. Royce?"

"Four, including myself."

"Without mentioning the disappearance of Mr. Baines' daughter, you can provide the description of Jack Foyle to your three fellow officers. Ask them to quietly make inquiries about Foyle, but if they manage to discover his whereabouts or see him, they are to take no action on their own, but report directly to you. Tell your men that you have had an inquiry through Scotland Yard regarding a man sought by the police in America who may have taken up residence in Kendal. That should satisfy any questions they might have."

Pitt turned to Baines. "Arthur, I think Fin and Jake should enjoy an evening at one or two pubs in town this evening. They needn't ask questions about Foyle but simply keep their eyes open for a man of his description. If they manage to spot him, they are simply to return here and inform you. You can then contact Mr. Royce and myself. I expect they will have to do the same tomorrow and the next evening so you will have to provide them with enough funds to pay for a few pints and a meal or two."

"Gladly," said Baines, "whatever is necessary."

"Fine. If they come by any useful information, notify me and Constable Royce immediately and we will meet here. I will ride back into town with Mr. Royce, check into the Riverside hotel and then see Hamish. If a wire from MacLeish arrives, as I think it will, read it so you know if and when he will be arriving tomorrow and then have one of your men deliver it to my hotel. I think Fin should meet the Inspector at the station if he arrives tomorrow as I expect. They know each other and Fin can fill him in with what we have learned so far. What have you told your house staff about your daughter's disappearance?"

"Only that she is gone. Nothing in connection with the Becker clan.

"Well, I am certain there is some speculation on their part but I do not think it wise to tell them you think she has been kidnapped just yet. They will know Mr. Royce of course, but you might explain MacLeish's arrival tomorrow as simply a visit by an old friend. You could tell your cook that you and Mary Fiona have had a disagreement over a personal matter and that she has gone off for a few days to spite you. That should be sufficient and believable. I am sure the cook will spread the word. You will have to tell Jake, of course, but caution him to silence in the matter."

Pitt paused for a moment, then turned to Fin. "When Inspector MacLeish arrives, bring him to Mr. Baines estate or to Hamish's tobacco shop, whichever he prefers. The shop was known as Welch Tobacconist but Hamish may have changed the name by now. At any rate, it is in the same location just off the town square. If the inspector prefers to come here after his long trip, then at least let me know he has arrived."

Upon arrival at the hotel, Pitt arranged for a room with private bath, sent a wire off to Elizabeth telling her where he was staying, then walked to Hamish's tobacco shop. An new oval sign hung from wrought iron over the door that read:

KENDAL TOBACCONIST
PIPES, TOBACCO, SNUFF & ACCESSORIES
Hamish MacLeod, Proprietor

He smiled as he walked in the door to the soft tinkle of an overhead bell, thinking that at least the shop name would not need changing if Hamish decided to sell in the future. The new proprietor was sitting on a stool behind the front display case, cup of tea at hand and a local newspaper spread out on the glass top. Pitt took a few steps forward and reached out to shake hands.

"You certainly look relaxed and quite the comfortable shopkeeper, Hamish."

Hamish smiled and stood as he reached out across the counter. "Aye, lad, it slows a bit this time of day so I take my afternoon tea. My busy times are midday and right before closing. Would you like a cuppa?"

"I would, that," replied Pitt, "and then I have a tale to tell you of a murder plot right here in Kendal."

Over tea and a small plate of biscuits, Pitt spent the next thirty minutes relating the details of the Baines case to Hamish, pausing only twice when customers entered the shop for tobacco. When he finished, he asked Hamish for assistance.

"Aye, lad, I will help in any way I possible but my time is limited because my daytime hours are spent in the shop."

"It is in the shop that I think you can be of help. You have the description of the three people we are looking for and if they come into the shop, you can notify me or Baines. In addition, I thought I might act as your employee several hours each day for the next few days and do the same. Edward Becker is the only one of the three we know for certain smokes tobacco so there is an off-chance he would stop in here for cigarettes if and when he comes to Kendal. Edward Becker is from the American south so his accent would give him away but the woman and Jack Foyle are originally from England and have probably reverted to their original voice, at least to some degree." Pitt paused, then went on. "There is also a personal reason. I would like to get to know the townsfolk. I have become engaged to a young woman who will soon be moving here as part of the staff of a new clinic. She is currently a sister at St. Bart's but will be in charge of the nursing staff once here. It is early days yet, but its possible I will be living in Kendal permanently in the near future."

Hamish smiled and reached out his hand to Pitt. "Well now, that is news to brighten my day. Congratulations, lad. And what might be the bonnie lass's name?"

"Langston, Elizabeth Langston, and bonnie lass is a fair description. She is tall, attractive, and with a wit to match my own. Unless you have other plans, sup with me at the Riverside Hotel this evening and I will tell you how I met her. By the bye, have you received the pipes I had sent from London?"

"Aye, that I have. Both the BBB and Comoy's pipes arrived a couple days ago and I received some Peterson pipes yesterday but I have put none of them on display as yet. Would you like to do that?"

"I would, and will do that now. It will give me an opportunity to become familiar with the shop." What he did not say is that it would also give him a chance to look through the new pipes for one or two he could give to Fin. The shop was composed of two rooms, the larger display room in front with a smaller one to the rear, though both were more than adequate. The storage and workroom at the rear had two workbenches, shelves, a couple large cabinets, a Chubb that was fixed to the floor, and a door that exited to a narrow alleyway behind the shop. There was also a loo shared with the cabinet maker next door.

Pitt went through the new pipes, selected six of each brand for display in the glass case at the front of the shop and arranged them neatly in three rows on a clean piece of green felt he found in one of the cabinets. He also selected two for Fin: a straight Comoy's and a bent Peterson, both of slightly more than five inches in length and with stout shanks that Fin could carry in a pocket with little fear of breaking. He then spent an hour looking over the stock of tobaccos that rested in closed bins on shelves at the rear of the shop. At one point, he asked Hamish how many glass tobacco containers he had in the front of the shop and was told he had six. When he finished, he returned to the front of the shop.

"I think you should increase your tobacco jars in the front to eight or ten and there are several pounds of tobacco on the shelves in back that are so dry and crumbled they are not recoverable. I marked the containers and you should simply throw the tobacco in the trash. Also, you need to replace the rubber seals on several of the glass tobacco bins before you replenish your stock."

"I will do that tomorrow," said Hamish. "The pipes you arranged in the front display case look fine. Is there anything else I should do?"

"Did Welsh have any contracts with the tobacco syndicate in London?"

"Not that I know of but I'll look through the paperwork he left."

"Well, if he had a contract in the past, you should renew it under the new shop name. If not, you should establish an account with them. In the meantime, get as wide a selection of tobaccos as you can from Samuel Gawith Tobaccos. Small amounts at first, perhaps two pounds each, and we'll see what is popular and what is not. Since Gawith is local, you can increase the stock of popular tobaccos in a day."

"Thank you so much, laddie. You've only been here a few hours and we're well on our way to being on sound footing." Hamish grinned. "I might be successful in this business yet."

Late in the afternoon as Pitt was ready to leave to return to the hotel, he set the pipes he had selected for Fin on the counter and told Hamish to add four ounces of tobacco to his account for the pipes.

"As you are an employee here, so to speak, and in return for your assistance," said Hamish, measuring out the tobacco, "you can have them at no charge, of course."

"No, in this case, Hamish, I will pay full price. They are a gift for a friend, though if for myself, I would accept. Meet me in the hotel bar about seven o'clock and we will have dinner." Pitt Paused. "Tell me a bit about Kendal, Hamish. I have visited several times but really know little of the area."

"Well, Laddie, 'tis a market town, but you know that. Primarily wool but also clothes, and shoes. And of course, there are two tobacco producers here, Samuel Gawith and Gawith Hoggarth, the Samuel Gawith company on Lowther Street being the oldest of the two, having been founded in 1852. Actually, Gawith took it over in 1852 from the original owner name Harrison. Both produce snuff and other forms of tobacco.

"It is and has been known as Auld Grey Town

by the locals because of the grey limestone used for so many of the buildings and homes. This shop and my cottage are built of it. The river Kent runs through the town, almost dividing it. It is a short stream with beginnings in the hills surrounding Kentmere and flows twenty miles or so into Morecambe Bay. Tis fine fishing for salmon and trout, as you might know. The public houses provide good beer, ale, food, and are generally quiet, but a couple pubs most often frequented by the lads at sheep shearing time are known to be rowdy at week's end. In all, tis a good place to live. Do you really think you may move here?"

"I am considering it. It is time I settled down a bit and began thinking about a family. We will talk more of it later."

The walk back to the hotel was a pleasant one. Though a cool afternoon, the sun was shining through swift moving, scattered clouds, throwing rapidly changing shadows on buildings and cobbled streets. Buds and small leaves were appearing on trees and spring flowers would soon be appearing in window boxes and poking through the earth. "I could live here," he mumbled to himself as he walked, and then reflected on the pleasant thought that if he did, fishing the River Kent would soon be on his agenda. Mayhap he could convince Mick to join him for a few days holiday if he could get away from his tobacco shop.

As he entered the hotel, the clerk motioned to him. Pitt walked to the front desk where the clerk handed two telegrams to him, saying. "The first arrived by messenger from Mr. Baines, and the second was just now delivered from the telegraph office, Mr. Pitt. If you have a reply, I can have one of the boys take it immediately." Pit read the first. It was from Inspector MacLeish.

Have arranged for three days in Kendal. More if developments warrant. Arriving by afternoon train tomorrow at two-forty. MacLeish

Below was a short hand written note from Baines saying he would have Fin meet the train. The second telegram was from Elizabeth. He glanced at it and then told the desk clerk there would be no reply to either but he would appreciate a pot of tea in his room, Assam, if they had it. Elizabeth would be arriving in two days, staying a fortnight, and then returning to London to make arrangements to transport her personal belongings to Kendal. She would be staying at the Riverside, the same as Pitt. He smiled at that and wondered if it was foreplanned or arrangements simply made after Bess received his wire. No matter, it was the bright point of his day.

His room was a large one with a sitting area toward tall lattice windows on the outside wall, hinged so they could be opened, and a corner fireplace opposite the door to the lavatory. The lavatory was done in white tile, well appointed with large oval tub, cabinet mirror and full length mirror hung on the linen door. Ovals of soap scented of lavender were placed at the basin and tub. He had a fondness for the fragrance, so picked one up and carried it to the writing desk near the fireplace.

His tea arrived just as he finished putting his

few clothes away and his Adams revolver in the reinforced inside pocket of his coat. The revolver, in spite of its weight, carried well in the leather lined pocket and did not produce a noticeable bulge. He poured himself a cuppa, then stood at the window looking out on the river Kent, watching the clouds reflected on the slow moving water; thoughts, both personal and professional running through his mind.

He did not have mixed emotions about his relationship with Elizabeth. The rapidity with which it developed might have left him amazed at first, but there was a rightness to it, a goodness to it; a feeling of something that ought to be. He did want a family, children, a nice place to live... and, he smiled, a dog. And that was that.

The Baines case puzzled him. Not the physical aspects of it. It was what it was: a planned murder, and murders were committed every day by individuals of every class all over the world. No, what puzzled him was that three people, admittedly with family connections, but with disparate backgrounds would would be so consumed with revenge after twenty years that they would risk everything to carry it out. Granted, the widow and ex-convict had a connection, but why Jack Foyle, the cousin and drunk? Pitt found it hard to believe that any plot Edward and Martha hatched would require a third party to carry it out, though if he were right about Foyle holding Mary Fiona, his presence was obviously convenient. But the kidnapping of Mary wasn't planned, he was certain of that. It was simply a matter of opportunity presenting itself, and Pitt suspected it would not have taken place had Jack

Foyle not been available to play his part. Foyle's reasons for his participation might be money, drink, or perhaps a relationship with Martha that was anything but pure as the driven snow.

One would think twenty years as a convict would give Edward Becker pause to commit a crime that would result in a return to gaol or a hangman's rope. And, in fact, Pitt's short and fruitless conversations with Edward seemed to indicate he was a reluctant player. It was obvious he was tempted by the substantial sum offered by Baines. Pitt was convinced it was Martha who was behind the plot. She apparently had the dedication of a zealot, a monomania to use the term of an alienist. Perhaps Martha had some carnal hold over both men. There were stranger things under the sun. It would be interesting to find out why, but perhaps they never would.

Pitt had been in the hotel restaurant but a few minutes and was sipping a pint of Guinness when Hamish entered, sat, and when the waiter appeared, ordered a pint of the same. They placed their dinner order when the waiter returned and then Hamish, as if there was some conspiracy to be shared, leaned forward with a smile.

"A'right, laddie, tell me about this Elizabeth of yours."

"We first met at St. Bart's when Inspector Angus MacLeish was shot..." Then Pitt went on to tell of her taking care of him when he was wounded several days later and meeting again in London just a week ago. He skipped any descriptions of her bedroom. At the end of his account, he added that he had been thinking for some time of settling down, getting married and raising a family. He added that if he moved from London, it would probably be to Kendal.

After a sip of Guinness, Hamish replied, "Ach, lad, 'twould be nice if you settled here. As I said earlier, Kendal is a market town, but a nice one nonetheless, with good people. Neighborly, you might say, always willing to lend a hand. Have you given any thought to what business you might take up?"

"Sheep, possibly." Pitt made it sound almost as a question.

"Bu' laddie, you've nowt experience..."

"No, but you have, and I'm sure I can find some experienced men who will be willing to help for a decent wage."

"True. Kendal is a major wool market and there are a lot of old hands. If you decide you want to raise sheep, I will ask around to some of the older chaps who have retired and would be willing to offer advice or even a spot of work. A word of caution though," Hamish said with a smile, "you may get more advice than you want. Sheep herders are opinionated."

After dinner they went to the bar for coffee, brandy and a pipe. Pitt had just passed his tobacco pouch to Hamish when a young constable came in and spoke to the barman who pointed to their table. He introduced himself as Constable Quinn and was relaying a message from Chief Constable Royce that no one answering the description of Jack Foyle had been seen or found as yet. Mr. Finny and Mr. Jacobs had been observed by himself at one public house but not approached. Pitt thanked him and told him to remind the Chief Constable that if he were needed immediately, he could be found at Hamish's tobacco shop during the day and at the Riverside Hotel all other times except when he was at the Baines residence. In case he were going to the Baines residence, he would notify the Chief Constable.

After another half hour's conversation, Hamish left for home and Pitt went to his room and to bed. It had been a long day and the morrow promised another.

WEDNESDAY, 8 APRIL 1896

It was a long day. Pitt went to the shop early in the morning and other than taking an hour to have a bite to eat and wander several of the streets nearby, his time was spent in the tobacco shop. His being there did give Hamish a chance to go home for lunch and he commented afterward how nice it would be to have Pitt around regular like.

"One thing, though," said Hamish, "While you were out for a bite to eat, a woman came in for some snuff and cigarettes. From her speech, she were undoubtedly English but what got my attention was she fitted the description you gave me of that Becker woman we're looking for. She even had freckles. Very faint, and might easily be covered with powder, but they were there. I tried to engage her in conversation, hoping you would return, but she were not the talkative kind. She left after a few minutes."

"Did you see which way she went?"

"No, another customer came in and I did not notice, though if she would have walked in front of the window, I would have seen her and I did not. She must have turned right toward the center of town."

"How long ago?"

"Soon after you left for lunch. About an hour."

"Damn! A missed opportunity."

"Well, we cannot be certain it was her."

"No..." Pitt pause for a moment to light his pipe. "But this is a deadly game of chance that could end for good or ill as a result of missed opportunities. There was nothing else you could do, of course, but if she comes in again and I am not here, try to learn her name."

"I will do that lad. Sorry."

Pitt smiled. "No need to be sorry, Hamish. You noticed her and I may not have. At least it reinforces my assumption that she is here in Kendal. That is something in our favor."

The remainder of the day was relatively quiet though they sold two pipes late in the day, a Peterson and a Comoy's, both with bent stems. Pitt was sitting on a stool at the front counter, sipping a cup of tea, when Hamish came from the back of the shop.

"We did well today, Hamish. Sold some cigarettes, snuff, a few cigars and some of the new pipe tobacco you put out. Two pipes as well. Do the chaps here prefer bent stem pipes?"

"I think it is about fifty-fifty. Most of my business is from lads who work for the mills and a bent stem pipe fits easy in a jacket or waistcoat pocket. They carry a pipe in one pocket and a pouch of tobacco in t'other. Some hire out at shearing time and then buy snuff or wide-cut tobacco to chew. They cannae shear and smoke at the same time. The shearers use a single or double bow shear that is near razor sharp and smoke in the eyes might mean the loss of a finger."

"I had not thought of that, but I guess not. Would you like to come to the hotel for dinner again this evening?"

"I think not, lad, but would you like to come to my place for a hearty stew tomorrow evening? We could pick up some tarts at the bakery on the way home as a treat after dinner."

"I would like that. We will plan on it and hope events do not keep us from it."

Before returning to the hotel, he walked a half mile or so along the river Kent thinking again that Kendal would be a good place to live, or even the smaller town of Burnside just to the north and also along the river. The Kent was a short river but he knew it to be a good fishing stream. He smiled to himself, then mumbled half aloud, "If I take up farming and a family, I suspect I will have little time for fishing." But I'll make time, he thought. And then, aloud again, "I wonder if Bess likes to fish?"

It was beginning to cool and grey scudding clouds were forming to the west as he walked back to the hotel. Rain before midnight, he thought, and probably cooler tomorrow. He had shepherd's pie with a half pint of bitter for dinner, then coffee and chocolate cake for dessert. The waiter warmed his coffee and he took it to the bar. Finding an empty table near the fireplace, he filled and lit his pipe, stretched out his legs to the fire and simply enjoyed the comfort along with the dull murmur of conversation that flowed around him. So much so, that he nodded off and only woke when the barman asked if he would like more coffee or something a bit stronger.

"A whiskey would be agreeable," said Pitt as he relit his pipe with a spill from the box next to the fender.

As the barman set a whiskey and small glass pitcher of water on the table he nodded toward the clock on the far wall. "Last call in forty minutes. If you would like one to take upstairs with you, let me know."

Pitt chuckled. "I may be abed by last call." And he was.

THURSDAY, 9 APRIL 1896

He had been right about the rain. Looking out the window upon rising, he could see clouds hanging low to the horizon and a steady, though light, rain falling. He completed his toilet, picked up his Barbour jacket and soft wool cap and walked downstairs for tea and scones before setting out for the tobacco shop.

There were few customers and mid morning found Hamish and Pitt sitting in chairs behind the front counter enjoying tea and a pipe.

"I hesitate to say," said Hamish, "but have you given any thought to the possibility of real mistreatment of Mary Fiona at the hands of the bastard that took her? I mean, he's a drunk and she's an attractive young woman."

"You mean sexual interference? Yes, I have thought of it and it is possible, maybe even likely unless Martha Becker forbids it. She seems to have a hold over Jack and Edward but whether it extends to the point of a drunken Jack having his way with Mary, it is hard to say. I do know this: If a sexual assault has happened, I doubt anyone will keep Baines from killing him." Pitt was silent for a moment and drew on his pipe. "I doubt I would try."

"Nor would I," said Hamish, pouring more tea. "I tell ya, lad, there is evil in the world, evil in some people, tha' nowt can be done with it than to excise it like one of those Harley Street doctors does with cancer."

"Yes... but sadly, it almost always grows back in one form or another, does it not?"

"Aye, lad, it does, but at least you have got rid of the original."

A customer, dressed in sheepskin vest and soft hat, came in and Hamish got up to greet him. "Hello Martin, lambs coming on yet?"

"A few, Hamish. 'Nother ten day or fortnight an' we will be knee deep. I heard ye'd taken over Welch's shop an' thought to come to town to say hello. An' to buy some snuff an pipe tobacco as well."

"We have some new tobaccos as well as pipes. Take a look around and if you see something you like, let me know. By the by," nodding toward Pitt, "this fellow is Joshua Pitt from London. He has come to help me out for a few days till I get my feet on the ground, so to speak. I knew his father and mother in the old days and have known Joshua since he was a wee lad."

Pitt stood and shook hands. "How many sheep do you have, Martin?"

"Nigh on ta four hundred bu' tha' will likely triple with lambing."

"And how much land..."

Hamish interrupted. "Joshua has been thinking of moving from London and possibly raising sheep. He means no to be prying."

Martin pointed at one of the Peterson pipes in the counter. "Could I see that pipe, Hamish?" He looked the pipe over, said he would take it and then turned to Joshua. "We have about two hundred hectares, more'n needed for ta sheep bu' we also have some Ayrshires and a few head of Angus tha' we graze."

"Thank you, Martin. I did not mean to pry in any way, but I truly am interested in raising sheep."

"Weel, lad, tis not an easy life, bu' a good one. If your heart is set on it, you might do well to hire out ta some herder and work with sheep for six months or so afore ya decide."

After Martin left, Hamish echoed his suggestion of working with sheep for some months before making a decision and Pit agreed. "It makes good sense, Hamish. After years of city life in London, I am not sure I would be cut out to be a farmer but it appeals to me."

It was late afternoon when the bell at the door rang and Pitt looked up from the newspaper he was reading to see Jake coming into the shop.

"Hello, Jake, is it news you bring, or tobacco you want?"

"A telegram, sir. Mr. Baines said you would want to see it immediately."

It was from Mrs. Keating, his landlady in London, and read:

Mr. Pitt. Coffin tells that a Mr. Becker quit the Blue Duck this morning giving no indication of his

destination but commented to the landlord that he was leaving London and glad of it.
Mrs. Keating

Pitt glanced up from the telegram. "No reply, Jake. Anything else?"

"Yes sir. Mr. MacLeish has arrived and said to tell you he traveled in the delightful company of a Miss Elizabeth Langston."

Pitt smiled. "I am sure they had much to talk about. Please tell Mr. Baines I will see him in the morning. How is he, by the by?"

"The strain is terrible on him, but bearing up, sir."

As Jake was leaving, Pitt thanked him, then turned to Hamish. "I am afraid I will have to forgo the remainder of the day in the shop. It is best I stay close to the hotel. And I will not be in the shop tomorrow morning due to meeting with Mr. Baines."

When Pitt returned to the hotel, there was a sealed note waiting for him at the desk. It was from Elizabeth, and short. "*Room 22. Dinner? Or...? Bess.*" He grinned. Her sense of humor was akin to his own and her room only a few doors along the hallway from his. He went to his room, washed, and then walked to her room and tapped lightly on the door. After several seconds, her voice came through the door.

"Who is it?"

"Inspector MacLeish's brother."

She opened the door and was in his arms before he could enter. Through a rather passionate kiss, he murmured, "Best we step inside, Bess, before we give the wrong impression to neighbors."

Stepping back, she laughed. "Or mayhap the right one." She stepped back and he closed the door. She was wearing a pale blue dressing gown that buttoned from hem to neck.

Pitt stepped back. "Not a few buttons, that."

"Undo the top few and it slips right off. It is what is worn underneath that is important."

"And what is that?"

"Nothing," she said with a giggle, leading him to the bed.

Afterward, she lay close with her head on his shoulder. "Have you made progress on the Baines problem?"

"Very little, I fear." Pitt went on to tell her of the kidnapping of Mary Fiona and that in spite of the efforts of the local constabulary with the help of Jake and Fin, she had not been located. "We believe she is still alive and will somehow be used in an effort to get to Mr. Baines." He paused for a moment. "We have no idea what condition she will be in when found, nor what might have been done to her. We may need your assistance when we find her."

"Of course. Whenever and wherever."

He kissed her on the forehead, then got up and began to dress. "Would you like an early dinner?"

"I would. I am famished." She rose, laid her robe over her arm, then turned to him. "Joshua, it is so good to be here with you... to be loved..."

He put his arms around her an kissed her neck. "I feel the same, lass, I feel the same."

After dinner, they moved to chairs near the fireplace in the bar for coffee and brandy. Pitt took a spill from the edge of the fender and lit his pipe. They sat quietly, arm to arm. Pitt, staring into the low flames, finally gave voice to what he was thinking. "I could live here, Bess, or someplace nearby. It is a good town with good people; a fine place to raise a family. I know not what I might do for a living but there is time to decide all that."

She turned to him. "You would not miss London?"

"I am sure I would. As jaded, corrupt, dirty, wet, smoke and fog ridden as it is, I love that city. There is something magical about it." He paused to smile. "But then, it is not all that far, is it? If we settle here, we could spend a few days in London as we wished and as we have time."

"And as the children get older, we could take them..."

He chuckled. "Planning a large family, are we?"

She took his hand and squeezed it. "I have no doubt, no doubt at all."

He took a sip of coffee. "Speaking of which, I suspect we should exhibit some discretion when meeting. It may be best to confine ourselves to your room rather than mine. Better I should be seen entering or leaving your room than the opposite."

"I suppose." She smiled. "But the maids will know, will they not?"

"Hmmm... Yes," he said, laughing. "They always do."

Pitt was in his room preparing for bed when there was a knock at the door. He opened it to find Fin standing in the hallway dripping water from the misting rain and fog.

"Come in, man. Have you learned anything?"

Fin, removed his cap and stepped inside the

room. "We didnae find the cove, gov, but may 'ave found the pub 'e favors. There be a small public 'ouse near the railroad yards called Black Boot. Fairly named, cause of the soot from the locomotives. Seems there be a chap who comes in irregular like, who sounds faintly English but uses American words at times. An' 'e fits the description. It were Jake who tumbled 'im, seein' 'e know'd the landlord an' bought 'im a drink."

"Does the landlord know where he lives?"

"No, bu' it cannae be far cause 'e comes afoot."

"Was he in tonight?"

"No, an' we stayed till last call. Didnae show, but the landlord said 'e was in the night afore, early, and brought a pitcher with 'im for beer. Drank two whiskey's an' poured two in the pitcher."

"That has to be our man, Fin! I have one more chore for you. Go by Chief Constable Royce's home, rouse him if necessary, tell him what you have told me and ask him to stop here at eight o'clock in the morning and we will travel to Baines' together. You might also add that Inspector MacLeish has arrived though, he may know that already."

"Aye, sor, I will do that." As he turned to leave, he paused. "I were tinkin' sor, ta man has ta eat an' I doubt he would wander far. An' ta young miss would need fed. I could visit some of the shops nearby ta rail yards come morning, ask a few questions..."

"Grand idea, Fin! Just grand. Tell Mr. Baines it was your idea and I wholeheartedly agree. If you could be back at the Baines' residence before noon to report it would be good but if you lay on to his track, take whatever time you need."

FRIDAY, 10 APRIL 1896

Pitt woke to a feeling of disquiet. He'd had a dream, or at least he thought it was a dream. He knew he was in bed, asleep, but still aware of his surroundings. But it was a dream, a dream of a faceless woman standing next to a faceless man, confronting Pitt. They were in a room that he had never been in before but he felt certain it was at Baines' manor. He thought at first the woman, who was in a rage, was screaming at him, but he soon realized she was looking past him, directing her offensive and hateful words at someone behind him. Both the woman and the man were armed with revolvers and Pitt knew he dared not turn to see who was behind him or he would certainly be shot dead. He felt helpless and hopeless. The woman stepped forward, raised her revolver, and at that instant, a side door to the room opened and Maggie, Baines' maid, stepped in to ask if anyone would like tea or coffee. And he woke.

It was one of those rare dreams that one remembers vividly upon waking and he felt certain that at least part of the solution to the Baines' affair could be found in the dream. But what it was, try as he might, he could not fathom. The dream preyed on his mind as he made preparations to go downstairs to meet the Chief Constable and he continued to turn it over and over, but to no avail.

The morning had arrived bleak and blustery, still drizzling rain. Through the front window of the hotel lobby, Pitt saw Chief Constable Royce alight from a trap and walk briskly to the front door. They nodded to each other as Pitt walked to the front desk to leave a note for Elizabeth asking her to accompany them should they discover the whereabouts of Mary Baines. Not knowing what condition the young lass would be in, but fearing the worst, he felt having a woman with them would be prudent. And all the better that Bess was a trained nurse.

As they climbed aboard the trap, Royce remarked, "No doubt about it, your man Fin has his wits about him. He told me of his plan to visit some of the shops near the Black Boot this morning."

Pitt smiled as he lit his first pipe of the day. "He is not my man, actually. He works for Arthur Baines, though I've known him quite a while. Truth told, he is pretty much his own man, but I will say this: I would trust him with my life."

Royce snapped his whip over the back of the horse and picked up the pace. "There be no better endorsement that that, Mr. Pitt, no better endorsement."

When they arrived at the Baines' estate, Inspector MacLeish and Arthur Baines, both with umbrellas, were waiting for them on the front steps. After shaking hands all round and a few words between MacLeish and Royce to renew their acquaintance they adjourned to Baines' library.

Baines took a cigar from his desk humidor and passed the humidor around. Royce took one but MacLeish and Pitt indicated they would smoke their pipes instead. Baines still had a haggard look but appeared to be more in control than when Pitt last saw him. As he lit his cigar, he rang for a maid. "Coffee or tea? Or if you prefer, there's whiskey on the sideboard."

Coffee got the vote for all except Royce who preferred tea, and when the maid appeared, Baines told her they would like coffee, tea, and some cakes or scones, whatever was available. He sat down behind his desk and turned toward Pitt. "Finn told me of his idea to question some of the local shop keepers and left early this morning for town. Damn good idea, I might add. That man is a diamond in the rough."

Pitt held a flame to his pipe and between puffs, replied that he had expressed the same sentiment to Constable Royce on the way to Baines' home. "I expect if there is any information to be had from any shopkeeper on the whereabouts of Jack Foyle, Fin will dig it out."

"Then what?" asked Baines.

"Then we will set a plan in motion to take him, but if Mary Fiona is with him, as I suspect she is, we will have to be cautious. Before we move, I will contact Elizabeth Langston, a nursing sister who is in Kendal. She will accompany us and see to any immediate needs your daughter may have. No doubt she has been fed but that may be all. And we have no idea what emotional or physical condition she may be in." Pitt refrained form adding that he hoped she was still alive and then continued. "If we take Foyle and free Mary, it may lead to other consequences. As much as Martha Becker may want to keep to her time table, she may decide to strike early if Foyle is arrested. I have also had word that Edward Becker has quit the Blue Duck Inn, indicating that he was leaving London. I have no doubt he is on his way here or perhaps has already arrived. Stubborn he may be, but he will do Martha's bidding and if she decides to make an attempt against you forthwith, Edward will comply and we will have two to deal with."

There was a knock at the door and a maid came in with a tray of coffee, tea, and cakes, set it on the sideboard and asked if there would be anything else.

"No, Maggie," replied Baines. "I'll ring if there is. Thank you."

She curtsied and left. Baines turned again to Pitt. "So what are we to do?"

Pitt turned from staring out the window and set his pipe in the ashtray. "There is very little we can do but be on our guard at all times. We do not know where Edward Becker is, we do not know where Martha is, and we can only hope we will discover where Jack Foyle and your daughter is. There are too many unknowns. We speculate on an early attack and prepare accordingly, but that is about all. I would suggest, however, that we should all be armed." He looked to MacLeish. "I know the Inspector is, as am I, but the Chief

Constable is not in the habit of carrying a weapon, nor are you, Arthur. Do you have a handgun?"

"I have several. One, a small Adams is in this desk."

"I urge you to carry it at all times. Mr. Royce?"

"Assuming the worst, I took the liberty of drawing a Webley from the gun-safe at the police station. It is in my coat pocket."

Everyone fixed themselves tea or coffee, as was their wont; everyone except Pitt. While the men discussed various scenarios and the possible rescue of Mary Fiona, Pitt again stared out the library window at the countryside, his pipe, though unlit, clenched in his teeth. The rain had stopped and a bit of sunlight was creeping through low scudding clouds. Contrary to his outward appearance of calm demeanor and control of what was an ambiguous situation, he was perplexed. The dream of early morning probably had much to do with it but he felt as though he were being led by events instead of being able to predict them with any certainty. The brutal reality of it was that he felt completely out of his depth. He walked to the sideboard, poured himself a half cup of coffee, then added a tot of whiskey in hopes it would clear his head and not fog it. When he walked back to the window, MacLeish moved next to him.

"You seem not yourself this morning, laddie."

"I am not, Mac. For certain, I am not. When this affair began, it was a matter of retribution for a perceived wrong. The threat, whether warranted or not, was justified in the mind of at least one who threatened. It was straight forward and could be dealt with accordingly. There were two options: Buy them off or meet them head on with force. The first failed. I opposed it but bowed to Baines' wishes. The first having failed, we could prepare for the second because we had a timetable. Granted, the day they intended to strike was one of several depending on how they calculated the 26 days they had given Baines but we could be ready. But then Mary Fiona was kidnapped. I refuse to believe that was part of the original plot, but more an opportunity they seized upon when it presented itself. Rescuing her is now paramount. Whatever else comes afterward is secondary for the time being."

"I have faith in Fin, lad. He will find her, never fear. He is like an old foxhound and will course the ground till he picks up a scent and then follow though. And you, lad, I have faith in you. You are not an investigator in the common sense, but more like a catalyst. You make things happen."

"I hope you are right, Mac... I think I'll take a walk outside to clear my head now that the rain has stopped. And I want to think about what approach we should take to rescue her."

Pitt set his cup on Baines' desk, pocketed his pipe and left, simply saying to Baines that he was going to take a short walk.

Beams of sunlight shown through breaks in the clouds as he walked along an uphill path past some outbuildings toward one of the pastures. When he arrived, he leaned against a wooden gate. There must have been sixty or more head of sheep in the pasture, a dozen or so near the gate, but they moved slightly away as he stretched out his hand toward them. All except one, a ewe heavy with a lamb or lambs. She came closer and nuzzled his hand. He was thrilled and pleased. He smiled as he thought maybe raising sheep was a better idea than he originally thought.

He was still standing at the gate a half hour later when he heard a shout. It was MacLeish. "Fin is back, lad, and he has found Jack Foyle. He is waiting for you to return to give us the details."

When they entered the library, Royce was standing at the sidebar, Baines was pacing back and forth, and Fin was sitting at Baines' desk sipping tea. He set his cup down and stood, addressing Pitt.

"I will not bother with all the shops I visited, gov, but eventually I stopped by a bakery shop run by a widow I know. 'Er name is Doyle. I told 'er who I was looking for, using the description you gave me, an' she said she thought it matched the looks of a fellow who comes in every few days. 'E does not talk much but she said 'e sounded American. I thanked 'er an' asked 'er not to say a word that someone was looking for 'im if 'e came in. She put 'er finger to 'er lips and smiled. I went two doors down from the bakery to a small tea shop, bought a cuppa an' a newspaper, an' sat at a table near the front window. Twern't five minutes an' widow Doyle appeared at the window, tapped, and pointed toward 'er shop. I nodded, left the tea shop an' without looking toward the bakery, crossed the street and sat on a bench in front of a cobblers. In a few minutes, 'e came out of the bakery an' walked toward the railroad yards. I followed some distance behind.

We walked past the yards an' 'e stopped in

the Black Boot for a few minutes, long enough for a drink, I 'spect. When 'e came out, 'e were carryin' a large jar of beer an' walked right past me. Ne'er gave me a look. I saunters after 'im, keepin' my distance. We only walked two blocks fore we came to a lane that runs for no more than three hundred feet off the main road. 'E went into the house at the end of the lane. It 'ud be a wee place, maybe three rooms, no more than four, and run down. I thought of takin' a peek in a window but decided it best not to an' came back here."

Banes was at the desk. "We must go immediately Joshua!"

Pitt turned toward him. "No, Arthur, we must not. Even though we have the police with us, we cannot take a chance that he would harm Mary if we break in. Aside from that, I want Miss Langston with us when we do. She is a trained nurse and we know not what condition your daughter is in. Let us give Foyle time to get drunk. If we are lucky, he will pass out or at least be so befogged that he will offer little resistance. We will go this evening just past dusk."

Pitt looked at Fin. You have done a fine job Fin, and I am sure Mr. Baines is appreciative. I know I certainly am. I would like you to be with us this evening."

"I wouldnae miss it, sor, I wouldnae miss it."

Jake was found in the barn and after harnessing a fast team to a four wheeler, was sent for Elizabeth. She arrived about ninety minutes later and Pitt told her of what Fin had found.

"But he did not see her?" she asked.

"No, and I am concerned for her condition. I am of the opinion these are brutal people we are dealing with and they care nothing for common decency. I suspect we will need your experience as a nurse and as a woman, Bess."

"You have both, of course. Will we bring her home?"

"I think that will be your decision. It would be better if we are able, but it is possible she may have to go to the clinic. Much will depend of her mental state as well..." He paused. "And if she has been interfered with."

"You do not think..."

"I do not know. But if she has been abused sexually, Foyle will never get out of that house alive. Police or no, Baines will kill him. And if he does not, I will."

Time passed slowly but at six o'clock, Pitt approached Fin and Jake. "Are the carriages ready?"

"Aye, sor," replied Fin. "At the front door."

"Alright, then, we will go. A leisurely pace, Fin."

Jake and Fin were each atop a four wheeler. Elizabeth, Pitt, and Baines in one carriage and Constable Royce and MacLeish in the other, they rode at a slow but steady pace into Kendal.

Pitt was lighting his pipe when Baines, exasperation in his voice, asked Pitt why they had to move so slowly.

Pitt glanced at Elizabeth then to Baines. "As I said before, I do not want to arrive till it is well dark, Arthur, and I want to give Foyle time to swill enough beer and whiskey that he is either asleep or befuddled enough that he is slow to move. If your daughter is there, as I believe she is, we want no further harm to come to her."

"Yes, yes, you are right of course. I am angry and pent up. When I get my hands on that bastard…" He looked at Elizabeth apologetically.

A slight smile appeared on her lips. "I have heard it before, that and worse. I understand how you feel, Mr. Baines, but you must follow Joshua's advice. It is the safest way for Mary."

Baines smiled in return, nodded his head, then sat back in the corner of the carriage.

The carriages stopped at the entrance to the lane. Fin and Jake tethered the horses and everyone gathered beside the front carriage. Fin pointed toward the end of the lane.

"It be the last house on the left, sor," he said to Pitt. "You can see a light through yon window bu' nae a light in the house next. It may be vacant."

Pitt turned to the group. "We will all go to the house next to Foyle's and you will wait there while I investigate. We need to know in what part of the house Mary is being held. That will determine what we must do next."

The distance from the empty house to Foyle's was about one hundred feet and Pitt crossed at an angle to the back corner. There was a small ramshackle porch with a rear door but no light in that part of the house. He went around to the far side and stopped next to a gritty window that a bit of light shown through. He peered in. He could see a wingback chair and a female figure in it who appeared to be lashed to the chair with several loops of rope. Though he couldn't see her face, he was certain it was Baines' daughter. He silently walked to the front of the house and at an angle, ten feet from the porch and single front window, could see Foyle sitting in a chair near the fireplace. A jar which had probably contained whiskey and beer lay on the floor and he appeared to be asleep. Pitt quietly returned the way he had come, going around the back of the house and then to the group gathered next to the empty house.

"I could not tell for sure if it is your daughter, Arthur, but a woman is in the back room tied to a chair. We have to assume it is Mary. Foyle appears to be asleep in the front room." He turned to Fin. "Jake, you and the Chief Constable go around back. MacLeish, Baines, myself and Elizabeth will be in front. When you get set, bang on the back door or smash through it. Either way, create a lot of noise. If Foyle wakes, it will distract him. As you do, we will go in through the front door.

They had no sooner stepped on the front porch when they heard a crash coming from the rear. Pitt took three steps and slammed into the door tearing it off it's hinges. His momentum carried him and the door several steps into the room. Foyle, a dazed expression on his face, was half way up from his chair when MacLeish flew past Pitt, grabbed Foyle by the front of his shirt, jerked him upright and slammed him into the wall. Baines rushed past into the short hallway and to the room off to the right.

"I need some light in here!"

Elizabeth turned up the wick on a small oil lamp that was sitting on a table next to Foyle's chair and carried it into the room, followed by Pitt, where they found Baines bending over a limp form in the chair.

Baines was mumbling. "Mary, Mary dearest, what have they done to you?"

The stench of urine and feces was almost overpowering. Baines' daughter may have been fed and given drink but never let out of the chair to wash or complete a toilet.

Elizabeth opened a small leather bag she was carrying and turned to the men. "Leave me with her. Go to the front room and I will call if I need you."

Pitt took hold of Baines' arm and steered him to the door. "Best we do as she says, Arthur. Bess will look after your daughter."

As they came into the front room, Baines took two steps, then leaped at Jack Foyle who was now being held by Constable Royce. The constable tried to pull Foyle back but Baines stiff armed him with his left hand and hit Foyle with a round house right knocking him out of the constable's hands and against the wall where he hung for a few seconds and then started a downward slide. Baines picked him up and hit him again. MacLeish started toward Baines but Pitt held him back, saying, "Once or twice more, then we'll stop him." Foyle was now down on the floor with Baines bending over him. He struck him once more, this time on the bridge of the nose and Pitt heard it break from across the room as he and MacLeish moved to get hold of Baines.

Loudly, Pitt said to Baines, "Enough for now, Arthur. We need him in condition to talk."

He then turned to Royce. "You, Fin and Jake, take him to your station, throw some water on him and get some coffee or strong tea in him. We'll be along as soon as we see to Mary."

The four of them left the house, Foyle being half carried and dragged the length of the road to the waiting carriage. Pitt turned to Baines. "No question but what the man attacked you, Arthur, and you did right by defending yourself."

"MacLeish nodded, smiling. "Aye, the lad is right. I saw it all."

Just at that moment, Elizabeth came to the hallway door. "We will need someone to get the carriage. She is semi-conscious and must go to the clinic."

MacLeish waved his hand and went out the front door at a run.

As Elizabeth was turning back to the room, she said, "If you two will help me, we can carry her into this room."

Pitt and Baines carried Mary Fiona into the front room and sat her in the chair that had been used by Foyle. Though Bess had cleaned her face, the odor that came from her was rank but no one said a word about it. Within moments, MacLeish arrived at the door with the carriage and they carried her to it. Once inside and settled, Bess turned to Baines.

"We'll take her to the clinic and I think you should stay for a bit while we get her cleaned up and to bed. Then you can see her for a few moments. I have given her something to make her sleepy and will give her another dose once in bed and at that time you can leave to go home. She needs rest and quiet. I can not be certain but from her vague mumbling responses to my questions I do not believe she had been interfered with. We will know more tomorrow."

"We will not be able to talk with her tonight, then." asked Pitt.

"No, certainly not tonight and I am not sure about tomorrow. She is in a state of shock and its is impossible to tell how deep it is. Doctor Redding will examine her and I am sure we will know more in the morning."

After the men had seen Mary into the capable hands of Bess and another sister, and Baines sat beside her bed for a few moments holding her hand, they took the carriage to the small police station at the north end of the city. The Chief Constable and the others were sitting around Royce's desk sipping tea when Pitt and the others entered.

"Not a word," said Royce. "We got two cups of coffee in him but he refuses to talk at all. Will not even give his name."

"Well, we know his name," Pitt replied, "but we need to know more."

Pitt, followed by Baines and MacLeish, walked back to the first of two cells located off a short corridor from the station's main room. Foyle was laying on the bunk, eyes open, staring at the ceiling. A rolled, bloody handkerchief was lying across the bridge of his nose.

"Foyle," said Pitt, "we need some information and I think it in your best interests to give it up."

Foyle shrugged and continued to stare at the ceiling.

"If you will not talk with me, I will open the door and let Mr. Baines try to persuade you."

Foyle turned toward Pitt and shrugged again.

Baines took a step forward. "Let me at the bastard! Just give me five minutes with him and he will tell us what we want to know."

Foyle turned his eyes back to the ceiling and said nothing.

"I think not, Arthur," said Pitt. "At least not now. Best we go back to your place and get some sleep if we are able. I suspect things will move quickly now and it would not surprise me if the days Martha Becker gave you in her letter will soon disappear when she discovers her cousin Jack has been arrested and their hostage released. We had better be in our best form come the morrow."

Foyle, who had overheard Pitt, turned his head toward him, smiled slightly and then turned his head back to stare at the ceiling.

As they started to leave, Pitt paused and turned back to Foyle. "What is Edward going to say, Foyle, when he finds the house empty? I suspect he warned your cousin Martha about leaving such an important task in the hands of a drunk."

Foyle's head snapped around and Pitt could see fear in his eyes. "I thought so," said Pitt, smiling.

As they stepped outside, Pitt turned to Royce. "There is a stand of bushes across the lane from the house that should provide sufficient cover for a watcher. Do you have a man that could be stationed outside Foyle's house tonight? "

"Aye, but no one to relieve him in the morning. And if Becker should arrive, should he try to arrest him?"

Pitt thought for a moment. "No, I think not. Becker is a hard man and would not stop at killing someone who made any attempt to hold him. Your man should observe but not follow if Becker leaves, as I am sure he will when he finds the nest empty. Your constable should then report back to you and then to us at Mr. Baines' home regardless of the time of night. I will ask Jake to relieve your constable at eight o'clock on the morrow if we do not hear from him in the meantime."

MacLeish, Pitt, and Baines returned to the residence in one carriage driven by Fin while Jake remained with the other carriage in Kendal. A moderate fog had settled in but there was no rain. There was little conversation on the way back and while Pitt and MacLeish lit pipes, Baines complained he had forgotten to bring any cigars. Pitt settled back in a corner of the carriage and stared out the window, though there was little to see with the fog. Not that he was seeing anything anyway. He was lost in thought and though his pipe was at his lips, it had gone out.

Fin took the carriage to the stables after they arrived and the three others went into the home and to the library.

Baines walked to his desk, selected a cigar from his humidor and lit it. "Would you gentlemen care to join me in a whiskey?"

Pitt, lighting his pipe, said, "A wee dram, with water," and MacLeish said the same.

Pitt was staring out the window as he had earlier but between the library's reflected light, the night and the fog, there was nothing that could be seen. No matter. His reflections were directed inward.

"Tell me, Arthur, how many hectare's would be needed to support two hundred head of sheep?"

Baines, obviously surprised at the question, thought for a moment before answering. "Well... I should think twenty hectares would adequately supply pasture for a hundred ewes and at least one-hundred-fifty lambs if additional silage or forage were provided. You could divide that amount of acreage into three sections and rotate the flock to them throughout the year." Baines smiled. "Are you seriously considering becoming a farmer?"

"Yes. Yes I am. I would like to marry and raise a family. As much as I love London, warts and all, I would prefer to raise children in the country rather than in the city."

MacLeish, who had been listening, had a shocked expression on his face. "You would be missed in the city, lad. More, I think you would miss the London, as you say, with warts and all. And so far as I know, you know nothing about farming or raising livestock of any kind."

"Quite true, Mac, on all counts. But I think it is something I must attempt. If I fail, I will have at least tried. And I fear not trying more than failing."

Baines set his drink on his desk. "If you are serious, Joshua, then you should consider raising cattle instead of sheep. It would require more land, of course, but in my opinion, sheep are a great deal more difficult for a novice, and a damn sight more work. Galloway, Angus, and Ayrshire cattle breeds do quite well here. There is one fellow in the district who keeps South Devons but I think that is more hobby than a serious market endeavor."

"How much land would I need for a herd that would support a family?"

"I think two hundred hectares would support one hundred twenty head of cattle, perhaps a few more."

"That is a lot of land, Arthur."

"'Tis moderate. There are many farms in the area of greater size." Baines paused and then continued. "When we have finished this Becker business, and if you are still serious about farming, come talk with me. I may have some ideas that would help."

Pitt finished his drink, tapped the dottle from his pipe and then turned to Baines and MacLeish. "It is almost midnight and I think time for bed, gentlemen. A few hours sleep would do us well. Arthur, would you ask one of your staff to wake us about six o'clock? That is if not woken sooner by one of Constable Royce's men."

"Yes, certainly," said Baines, "but I'm not certain I shall sleep."

Pitt smiled. "Then rest as you can. Good night."

SATURDAY, 11 APRIL 1896

Pitt woke to tapping at his door. The voice of one of Baines' male servants told him it was just six o'clock. Pitt thanked him and sat up on the edge of his bed. He was surprised at how quickly he had drifted off and also that his sleep had been dreamless. He fell asleep thinking that perhaps he would have a repeat of the vivid dream from the night before but it had not happened. Slipping on his robe, he picked up his small leather satchel that held his razor and soap, then went down the hallway to the bathroom.

He bathed, shaved his neck below his beard line, and then returned to his room to dress. Before putting on his tweed jacket, he put his pistol inside the waist of his pants just forward of his left hip. Though right handed, he found it more comfortable and quicker to reach across to his left than to carry it on his right hip or in a pocket. Unused to it as he was, it felt heavy but 'twas better to play it safe.

Coming downstairs, he realized he had no idea where breakfast might be found or served. There were rooms, both left and right, off the main hallway and he simply walked toward the rear of the manor hoping to find someone or at least encounter the aroma of coffee or bacon. He discovered both at the last door on his left.

It was a very large dining room and he realized after he entered that one of the doors he had passed also exited to the hallway. There was a large sideboard with food, coffee and tea set up at the far end and a doorway off to the left of the sideboard that Pitt assumed went to the kitchen or service room. MacLeish was already seated at another long table in the center of the room, full plate and steaming coffee in front of him.

"Good morning, Lad. Sleep well?"

"Soundly, at any rate. Where is Arthur?"

"'E were here a moment ago but one of 'is maids came in and announced that 'e 'ad a visitor so he went to see who it was."

Just at that moment, as Pitt was pouring himself a cup of coffee, Baines came into the room followed by a young constable. "Joshua, this is Constable Lucas Taylor who spent the night across from Foyle's house. He says a man visited the house about two hours ago."

Pitt set his cup on the table. "Tell me about it, Constable."

"Yes sir. Just before dawn, a man came down the street and knocked on the door of the house I was watching. Getting no answer to his knock, he tried the door and finding it unlocked, went inside. After a moment, I heard a crash as if he had thrown something against a wall and then he came out. He went back the way he came, almost at a run. I did not follow him, sir, as I was instructed not to."

"Quite so, but you did report to Chief Constable Royce?"

"Yes sir. He said to tell you Mr. Foyle continues to remain silent and that he, that is, the Chief Constable, will be here mid morning. He also added, sir, that he had no word from the clinic but I do not know what he meant by that."

"Ah... Mr. Baines daughter is in the clinic. Excellent job, constable. I take it you have had nothing to eat since last night?"

"No sir."

Pitt turned toward Baines but before he could say anything, Baines took the constable by the arm and lead him to the sideboard telling him to choose whatever he wished. He then turned to Pitt. "Jake drove the constable here. Should I have him stable the horses or return to town for the Chief Constable?"

"Hmmm... stable the horses, and then he can return to town with Royce's trap that was left here when we went to Foyle's place in your carriages last evening. Royce will want to use his own trap and Jake can return with him."

Baines left the room to tell Jake while Pitt joined the constable at the sideboard. He filled his plate with bacon, eggs, and a scone, had a few words with the constable, then walked toward the table to join MacLeish who was just standing, obviously with a refill of his plate in mind.

They were both still standing when a loud crash of crockery came from the kitchen and a deep male voice hollered, "Get out of my way, bitch!"

Through the kitchen archway came two individuals, the maid Maggie, and Edward Becker. Both were holding revolvers. And just as in Pitt's dream, she was looking right past him, her face twisted in hatred. But in his dream, she was faceless, not Maggie. In a flash, he put it together, Martha Becker was Maggie and she had been a maid in Baines' household for weeks. Baines must have entered the room because she continued to look beyond Pitt and spoke.

"You right bastard! Got your daughter loose, did you? Well, no matter. That little whore will be an orphan in a few minutes. You are going to pay for killing my husband Edwin with your own life."

A distraction, thought Pitt, we need just one second's distraction. It was not what he expected but MacLeish cleared his throat and spoke.

"From what I know, madam, you have little room to talk of whores."

She literally screeched and turned her pistol toward MacLeish. At that moment, the constable, who had gone unnoticed because he was out of their line of sight as they entered the room, threw his loaded plate at them.

It hit Edward Becker on the shoulder and as he started to turn, Pitt drew his revolver and fired at Maggie. The bullet hit her high on the left shoulder and she turned sharply, firing her pistol as she did so. The bullet from her pistol hit Edward in the neck. He clasped his throat with his free hand, gagged, and then dropped to his knees before falling face forward onto the floor.

Maggie swung her pistol in Pitt's direction but he fired a second time just a split second behind MacLeish who had drawn his pistol when the constable threw his plate. Both bullets hit her, one in the stomach and the other in the chest. She staggered two steps backward and then folded forward, collapsing on the floor.

In the few seconds of silence that followed, Pitt and MacLeish just stared at each other. MacLeish shrugged his shoulders, then moved forward to check on Edward Becker and Pitt turned to see Baines, head down, leaning against a chair. Pitt went to him.

"It is over, Arthur. It is over."

Baines looked up. "Jesus, Pitt! Maggie! It was Maggie! Here in my house the whole time."

"I should have suspected something like this, Arthur, but I did not. I had a strange dream that included Maggie but it led me nowhere. And if your daughter had not been in a severe state of shock, she could have told us, I am sure. But it matters little now. The danger is past. Jack Foyle will swing for his part in it and these two are gone."

MacLeish walked over to them. "Both dead, but Becker managed to gasp a few words. I could just make out, 'Should have taken the money.'"

Pitt, with a hint of a smile, said, "I am glad they did not. Had they taken it, I'm convinced the threat would have continued, if not immediately, then when they ran out of money or simply changed their minds. Also, Arthur, I think you owe Constable Taylor more than a meal. Had he not thrown his breakfast plate, we would have not had the couple seconds we needed to stop them."

Baines moved a couple steps toward the door. Constable, would you care to join us in a drink?" Turning to Pitt, he smiled. "Not too early, is it?"

Pitt, took his pipe from his pocket, put a match to the bowl and grinned. "In this case, Arthur, I think not... I really think not."

Epilog

Mary Fiona came home three days later, subdued, withdrawn, but responded in strong voice when spoken to. She was accompanied by Elizabeth who planned to spend the night and following day with her before returning to her duties at the clinic. Mary had not been interfered with sexually but had been slapped any number of times during the first two days of her captivity because she refused to eat. Though she finally accepted food and drink, fed by Jack Foyle, she had never been allowed from the chair she was tied to in order to relieve herself. Doctor Redding suspected the embarrassment of that had been every bit as traumatic as the kidnapping, so prescribed long walks and as much conversation as she could be prompted to participate in.

Arthur Baines had settled an award of £10,000 on Pitt for "services rendered," as he put it, in addition to a 100 hectare parcel of land that included a large cottage. Joshua could raise sheep or cattle, whichever he chose, though after talking further with Baines, he decided that cattle would be his preferred choice. Baines only proviso for the land was that if Joshua ever decided to leave permanently within five years, that the land would revert to Baines. After five years, the holding would pass to Joshua.

Joshua and Elizabeth set a late June wedding

date and Joshua returned to London to make arrangements for the permanent move to Kendal, much to the dismay of his landlady, Mrs. Keating. She was heartened, however, when he said that he wanted to keep his London rooms for at least a year and would pay her for the year in advance. He had given it some serious thought and decided if he had to come to London on business or if he and Elizabeth were to visit, his old rooms on Baker Street would provide a familiar place to stay.

In addition to settling his affairs while in London, he met with Coffin and offered him a position of general dogsbody on his new farm which Coffin accepted with alacrity, asking only if there were a tobacco shop nearby. Pitt assured him there was a fine shop in Kendal run by an old Scot named Hamish who would take care of his needs.

The comment about tobacco prompted Pitt to visit Mick at Bradley Tobacconists for conversation and a pound of Arcadia before his return to Kendal. Mick was sorry to lose a good customer but happy to hear Joshua was going to marry and move on to a more sedate life. They both laughed when Joshua remarked he did not know how sedate raising cattle and children would be.

Three days later, he was back at Baines manor and spent a cool but sunny afternoon walking the perimeter of his new property. Baines had been right. It was rocky in spots with limestone jutting out in some places but overall, good grazing land for livestock. He would need help and expert guidance but Baines would provide some assistance along those lines. Another man in addition to Coffin would be necessary as well and as much as he would like to ask Fin, he knew Baines had come to depend greatly on him. Mayhap he could borrow Fin from time to time. He smiled at the thought...

By late afternoon he was standing on the wide, partially enclosed portico that ran across the entire front of the cottage, gazing out over what was now his land. He would get used to it in time, he was certain, but for now, it was an odd feeling, an unfamiliar feeling. It wasn't *home* yet, but soon would be once he and Bess filled it with furniture, and children in the next few years if they were so blessed. For now, Bess would stay in Kendal for those days she was scheduled at the clinic and Pitt would work at making the cottage pleasant and habitable.

He knew he would miss London. More than that, he knew also he would miss the varied and sometimes adventurous life as an enquiry agent in that great city. He would miss the occasional conversations and dinners with other agents, rare as they were, and the irregular evening chess matches with Mick after he closed his tobacco shop, but that was behind him now. Or was it...?

END